ADVENTURE IN THE
DUNGEONS OF DOOM!

"I think it's gone!" Driskoll shouted ahead.

"I don't care," said Moyra, who had somehow found herself in the lead. "I'm not stopping until we're back home. Zendric will have to figure out how to save his soul on his own."

The words had barely left Moyra's mouth when she barreled headlong into a fur-covered wall. She bounced back hard enough to land flat on her back. Her eyes widened as she saw just what it was that she'd run into.

The owlbear was faster than Driskoll had guessed, and it knew the dungeon's maze far better than the kids ever would. It stood there before them, panting out its foul breath as it glared down at them with its crimson eyes.

BOOK I

SECRET OF THE SPIRITKEEPER

MATT FORBECK

BOOK 2

RIDDLE IN STONE

REE SOESBEE

BOOK 3

SIGN OF THE SHAPESHIFTER

DALE DONOVAN AND LINDA JOHNS

(October 2004)

BOOK 4

EYE OF FORTUNE

DENISE R. GRAHAM

(December 2004)

SECRET OF THE SPIRITKEEPER

MATT FORBECK

KNIGHTS
OF THE
SILVER
DRAGON

BOOK 1

COVER & INTERIOR ART
EMILY FIEGENSHUH

MIRROR
STONE

Secret of the Spiritkeeper

©2004 Wizards of the Coast, Inc.

Cover art by Emily Fiegenshuh
First Printing: August 2004
Library of Congress Catalog Card Number: 2004101143

9 8 7 6 5 4 3 2 1

US ISBN: 0-7869-3143-4
UK ISBN: 0-7869-3144-2
620-96530-001-EN

U.S., CANADA,
ASIA, PACIFIC, & LATIN AMERICA
Wizards of the Coast, Inc.
P.O. Box 707
Renton, WA 98057-0707
+1-800-324-6496

EUROPEAN HEADQUARTERS
Wizards of the Coast, Belgium
T Hofveld 6d
1702 Groot-Bijgaarden
Belgium
+322 457 3350

Visit our website at **www.mirrorstonebooks.com**

To Marty, Pat, Nick, Ken, and Helen

Special thanks to Nina Hess, Steve Winter, and Peter Archer

CURSTON

1. CATHEDRAL
2. THE WESTGATE
3. THE OLDGATE
4. DRISKOLL AND KELLACH'S HOME
5. MOYRA'S HOME
6. ZENDRIC'S TOWER
7. THE SKINNED CAT
8. WATCHER'S HALL

BROKEN TOWN

WIZARDS QUARTER

MAIN SQUARE

PHOENIX QUARTER

NEW QUARTER

TO RUINS

N

CHAPTER

1

"Curse it, boy!" Zendric said. "Put that thing down!"

Kellach nearly dropped the small, transparent ball.

Tall and thin, he looked like a fourteen-year-old scarecrow dressed in stained apprentice's robes. The know-it-all look he normally wore on his face vanished.

Zendric stalked over and snatched the shiny globe from Kellach's hands.

"Fool!" the wizard said. "You have no idea the danger you're toying with!"

Driskoll, Kellach's twelve-year-old brother, stood by the doorway. He had arrived moments ago to walk Kellach home from his lesson. Now he wished he had been a little late.

Zendric hoisted the globe up to the light streaming in through one of the tower's many windows. The globe was filled with murky smoke, and its golden bands glinted in the sunshine.

"If you never teach me anything, then how am I to know better?" Kellach said. He stepped up to the wizard's face, nose to nose with the old elf. "I've studied with you for two years, and I barely know how to light a fire!"

The wizard snorted and turned away. He carefully set the globe back into its place on the mantle. "I've told you this globe is off-limits. If you would spend as much effort on your lessons as you do on irritating me—"

Zendric bit his tongue. He turned back to face Kellach.

"Kellach, you are the most promising student I've ever had. But if you can't learn to respect such things of power, how can you be trusted with difficult spells? If Jourdain—"

"You leave my mother out of this!" Kellach poked Zendric in the chest.

Zendric stopped cold. He looked down at Kellach's finger, the tip of which still pushed against the wizard's robes. When his head came back up, his eyes were filled with wrath.

"You ungrateful whelp!" Zendric said. "I don't care how good a friend Jourdain was. You are never to cross my threshold again!"

"But you're my teacher," said Kellach.

"Not any more!"

Zendric chanted something quick and angry. Energy crackled through the air. Driskoll could feel the hairs on the back of his neck stand on end. Kellach backed away, stuttering an apology, but it was too late.

An invisible force lashed out and punched Kellach flat in the chest, driving him straight out the door.

Zendric growled in frustration, turned around, and headed straight for Driskoll. The boy froze for a moment, then tried to scramble under a desk. Zendric grabbed him by the collar and hauled him to his feet.

The wizard glared down at Driskoll. He shoved Kellach's pack into Driskoll's arms.

"Do your brother a favor, lad. Keep him away from here. The next time I won't be so kind."

With that, Driskoll found himself out on the street. He turned around to protest on his brother's behalf, but before he could utter a word the thick, ironbound door slammed in his face. He heard the lock fall into place.

Driskoll looked back around to see Kellach sitting on the cobblestone street, gaping at the wizard's tower. Driskoll shook his head. He walked up to his brother and handed him his pack.

"You've really made a mess of it this time," Driskoll said.

"Shut up." Kellach stood up, shouldered his pack, and started walking west. Driskoll followed close on his heels.

"Wait until Dad hears about this," Driskoll said.

Kellach didn't turn around. "You're not going to tell him."

It was all Driskoll could do to keep up with his brother until they reached Main Square. During the peak of the day, Main Square was the busiest place in all of Curston. Dozens of merchants kept tents and booths here, selling their merchandise to anyone in need or want of their wares. Now, though, the place stood nearly empty, with the exception of a few rows of booths kept by the richest merchants. Only two remained, haggling with a group of stragglers before shutting down business for the night.

Just beyond the booths, at the center of Main Square, stood a white marble obelisk, the most recognizable landmark in town. The obelisk rose thirty feet into the air, straight out of the center of a massive design in the square's pavement. The design allowed the obelisk to function as part of a humongous sundial.

The surrounding buildings cast long shadows over the square. The Cathedral of St. Cuthbert of the Cudgel soared above them all, its bell tower stabbing even higher than the top of Zendric's distant home. Atop the bell tower's peak, the circled cross of St. Cuthbert looked down over the square, like the eye of the demigod himself, searching for any incursion of evil.

The sun's rays caught the large rubies in St. Cuthbert's cross and set them ablaze. Driskoll glanced at the sundial. It would be less than an hour before all of Curston lay blanketed in darkness.

"Come on, Kellach," Driskoll said. "We'd better go home."

"I'm not going home." Kellach set his jaw.

"What are you going to do, join a group of fortune hunters and head for the ruins?" Driskoll laughed.

Kellach had often mentioned such plans, but only in jest. Centuries old, the ruins lay a few miles outside of Curston. Once the most prosperous city in the region, the ruins now lay deserted, with the exception of the occasional group of treasure hunters. Five years ago, one such group had broken a seal deep in the dungeons beneath the ruins, releasing hordes of demons and things viler still. The incident had nearly destroyed neighboring Curston. Even five years later, everyone had to be on guard against evil beasts from the ruins wreaking havoc on the town.

"The ruins," Kellach muttered. "That's not a bad idea."

"You're cracked," Driskoll said. "It's nearly curfew already. No one stays outside after dark."

"That's a legend they tell to scare children." Kellach looked at his brother pointedly as he emphasized that last word. "People walk the streets of Curston at all hours. Dad spends the night out here all the time."

"He's the captain of the watch," Driskoll said. "That's his job. Besides, he's surrounded by other watchers."

Kellach didn't seem to hear him. "Forget about fortune hunting," he said to himself. "I can be a modern Knight of the Silver Dragon instead."

"What are you babbling about?"

Kellach snapped his attention back to Driskoll. "Zendric used to talk about the Knights of the Silver Dragon all the time. He was one of them. They were founded back when Curston was still called Promise, in the town's early days."

Driskoll rolled his eyes. "Thanks for the history lesson."

Kellach ignored him. "The wealthy merchants of the town formed the Knights as a group of honorable warriors. Their job was to protect the city from outside threats."

"If they were so amazing, where are they now?"

Kellach shrugged. "Over the years, they slowly faded away. The last of them disappeared just after the Sundering of the Seal."

"So you want to model your career after a bunch of people who went missing?"

"Why not? If they were still around now, they'd be begging me to join them. You heard Zendric call me his best student ever. Plus, there's not a part of Curston I'm afraid to walk through. I know this town like the back of my—*oompf*!"

Someone ran headlong into the boys, knocking them both to the ground. They were a tangle of arms, legs, and heads. Driskoll's eyes landed on the person's face, and he recognized her instantly.

"Moyra!" he blurted as he pulled himself free. The girl— who was barely a year older than Driskoll—wore simple but well-used clothes, chosen to be the same gray color as the stones used in most of Curston's buildings. The idea was to help her blend in. But more often than not, it failed miserably, due not so much to the clothes as to the person wearing them.

Moyra's face was flushed, and she was breathing hard. She rolled off of Kellach and landed nimbly on her feet. As she did, she let loose a string of curses that would have made Zendric blush. "And thanks to you, I'm dead!" she finished.

As Kellach and Driskoll got to their feet, Moyra finally saw their faces, and she lit up like a lamp. "Boys! It's you! Thank the gods!" She threw her long arms around the brothers.

As Moyra pulled back from the embrace, a herd of footsteps came thundering toward them.

"From the sound of things," she said, calmer now, "it seems I could use your help."

CHAPTER

2

Before Kellach and Driskoll could respond, Moyra spun around behind them, grabbed their arms, and thrust the boys in front of her. They tried to squirm out of her grasp, but she just held them tighter.

"Hold still! You two can handle this. Once Kruncher gets a look at Kellach's robes, he'll turn tail and run like there's an owlbear on his heels!"

"Kruncher?" Driskoll asked, wrenching his arm free. "You're insane!" He tugged on Kellach's arm. "We have to get out of here."

"Who's Kruncher?" Kellach asked.

"Ask him yourself," said Moyra, pointing between Kellach and Driskoll's shoulders. The boys turned as one to find the largest person they had ever seen.

Driskoll had never met Kruncher, but he'd heard enough stories to recognize him on sight. Most of those tales started with someone running afoul of Kruncher and ended with that same person being beaten nearly to death.

Kruncher stood almost six and a half feet tall, and he was as wide as a barrel. His features supposedly favored those of his orc father, although from all reports his human mother was even uglier. His skin was the green-gray of a decaying corpse and he wore his coarse, black hair cropped short. His piggish nose turned up sharply at the end. Driskoll wondered if he could see straight through the nostrils into the half-orc's pea-sized brain. A single tusk stabbed out of Kruncher's lower jaw, on the right side of his mouth, lending him a perpetual sneer.

Four other half-orcs fanned out behind Kruncher, ready to cut off any escape. None of them were as large or as foul-featured as their leader. But any one of them could have thrashed Moyra and the boys without breaking a sweat.

Driskoll glanced around, looking for help, but the square was deserted. The few vendors that had been closing their stands had disappeared at the sight of Kruncher. Moyra and the boys were on their own.

"What's this?" Kruncher said. "Rabbit has friends?"

"Folk like we are friends to all," Driskoll said, with a quick bow to Kruncher and his fellows. Without a word, Kruncher raised his fist and chucked the boy under the jaw. Driskoll went down on his rump.

"Got 'nuff friends," he sneered. The half-orcs behind him laughed. One of them began to crack his knuckles.

"Rabbit not my friend," Kruncher said, pointing at Moyra. "Rabbit got my gold."

The boys turned to look at Moyra, whose attempt to hide behind Kellach's robes wasn't fooling anyone. She shrugged. "It's just one little coin," she said, "and I won it from him fair and square!"

8

Kellach turned back toward Kruncher and raised himself to his full height. Even so, the bully towered over him. "Is this true?" he asked.

"Is true," Kruncher admitted. Then he smiled wide, baring his broken teeth. "But still my gold." The thugs behind him nodded.

Kellach reached behind his back and grabbed Moyra's hand. He began chanting quietly.

"This is one of the most powerful wizards in all of Curston," Driskoll warned Kruncher. "If you value your life, you'd do well to leave now."

The thugs behind the lead bully tensed for a moment, but Kruncher never flinched. "Mighty wizard? Wears 'prentice robes? You funny!" With that, he bent over and began to laugh. The rasping sent a shiver down Driskoll's spine.

Driskoll looked to Kellach for a signal to run. But Kellach was watching Kruncher, staring right into his mouth.

"Hold still for a moment, would you?" Kellach asked the half-orc.

Kruncher stopped laughing, stunned that anyone had the nerve to interrupt his fun.

"Yes," said Kellach. "I see it now for sure. Amazing!"

Kruncher leaned over, curious now. Kellach never took his eyes off Kruncher's mouth.

"What?" Kruncher asked.

"What you've been so worried about, of course," Kellach said. "Come closer."

Kruncher leaned over farther until he and Kellach were nearly nose to nose. Kellach's right hand swung up to Kruncher's mouth and darted right in. Kruncher was so surprised, his jaw

9

fell open, and Kellach was able to snatch his fingers back before the half-orc's mouth snapped shut.

Kruncher stood straight back up. He began to snarl something at Kellach when he stumbled to a halt. There, right in front of him, Kellach held a gold coin in the air. "It's a bit worse for the wear, of course," he said, perhaps a bit too pleased with himself. "Do you ever bother to clean that mouth of yours? They sell some wonderful sticks for just that, only three booths down."

Kruncher let loose a bellow. He drew a long knife from a sheath on his belt. But before the furious bully could attack, Kellach took the coin, jumped as high as he could, and shoved it into the air—where it stuck.

Kruncher gaped at the coin. As he watched, the coin rose higher and higher into the air. He jumped for it, but it was just out of his reach.

Kellach turned to Moyra and Driskoll and whispered, "Run."

As Moyra and the boys sprinted out of the square, Driskoll looked back to see Kruncher grabbing one of his friends and tossing him up into the air. The thug plucked the coin from the air, but no one bothered to catch him on his way down. His head cracked on the cobblestones when he reached the ground.

Kruncher snatched the coin from his pal. "Get them!" he growled.

Moyra and the boys had a good head start on the thugs. But the half-orcs' legs were far longer. A half-head shorter than even Moyra, Driskoll had to pump his legs twice as fast as Kruncher to stay ahead of him. Their only hope was to find a safe harbor—and fast.

"Follow me!" Kellach said. Kellach led Driskoll, Moyra, and their pursuers through a seemingly random series of turns, dodging through alleys and racing down streets. As the procession ran on, the buildings became progressively more dilapidated. Driskoll realized in an instant where they were headed: Broken Town, Curston's seediest quarter. If Driskoll hadn't been so terrified of the thugs chasing them, he wouldn't have followed St. Cuthbert himself into this part of town, especially as late in the day as it was. Curston was a town of many curses, and they all seemed to gather in Broken Town for a festival every night.

More than once, Driskoll was sure that they had lost the thugs. But each time they slowed down for a moment, Kruncher rounded the corner just behind them and the chase was on again.

After a while, Driskoll shouted to Kellach, "Why can't we lose them?"

Kellach looked back at his brother, a lopsided grin on his face. "Who said we were trying to lose them?"

Before Driskoll could reply, Kellach put on a burst of speed, and it was all Driskoll could do to keep up with him. Off in the distance, Driskoll heard the bells in the cathedral ringing, signaling the official start of curfew.

Kellach pulled up short in a blind alley. He had led the group into a dead end.

"Kellach, are you out of your mind?" Driskoll said. He looked about wildly for any means of escape.

There were two doors that let out into the alley. Moyra grabbed the top of one of the doorjambs and hauled herself on top of it. She stood with the tips of her toes along the narrow ledge and hugged the wall, doing her best to blend in.

Driskoll tried the door handles, but both of the doors stood solidly locked. He couldn't reach the top of the door. There were no pipes or trellises to climb, no sewers or basements into which he could duck. It was a fine trap his brother had led them into.

Kruncher and his thugs dashed into the open end of the alley. Kruncher grunted. In the dying light, his wide, yellow smile seemed all the more menacing, and his eyes glowed redder than ever.

"Good run," he said, not breathing hard despite the chase. "Good hunt ends with good beating—or good death." His smile grew impossibly wide.

Driskoll stepped out in front of his brother. He flung his arms wide in as friendly a gesture as he could muster. "Come on, now, fellows," he said, struggling to keep his voice from cracking. "Can't we talk this out?" He smiled so hard he thought his face would split.

Kellach shoved Driskoll aside and stood face to face with Kruncher. "You brainless moron," he said.

"Um, Kellach," Driskoll whispered. "It's usually best not to make a madman even madder."

"Mor-on?" Kruncher mouthed the unfamiliar word.

"It's a synonym for other appropriate words, like *stupid, idiot,* and *fool.*"

"Sin-o-nim?" Kruncher said slowly. "Don't know that word. Don't like the others." He squinted at Kellach. "Don't like you. Hunt's over. Fun time now."

Kellach started backpedaling, but there was little of the alley left to go. As Kruncher closed the distance, Kellach looked up at Moyra and winked. She let loose with a scream that made the half-orcs flinch.

Seeing his chance, Driskoll leaped forward and swung his fist into Kruncher's gut with all his might. Kruncher let out a low, rumbling laugh. Driskoll pulled back his hand and rubbed it along the knuckles. Before he could say a word, Kruncher's arm shot out and punched him flat across his nose. He went sprawling backward.

Moyra screamed again. Driskoll grabbed his nose to see if it was broken. It was bruised but not demolished. The blood that poured from it was already stopping, but it still looked like Driskoll had nearly been killed.

Driskoll looked up to see Kellach standing near Kruncher. "That's enough!" Kellach shouted. "The lot of you are in grave trouble!"

Kruncher threw back his head and laughed. "Funny boy," he said. "For that, you might live."

The half-orc stepped forward and lashed out like a striking cobra, his hand catching the boy by the throat. Kellach struggled valiantly, trying to pry the steely grip from his neck. As Kellach fought for breath, Kruncher lifted him from the ground with one arm, keeping the boy at arm's length.

Kellach's legs kicked frantically. "If you have half a brain, you'll put me down," he rasped. "Now."

"Who gonna make me?" Kruncher said.

"We will," said a voice from behind the half-orc.

Kruncher's sneer melted. Still keeping Kellach suspended in mid-air, he slowly turned his head to find a full patrol of watchers standing behind him, their blades drawn.

The sergeant in charge of the patrol—a swarthy, barrel-chested dwarf with a salt-and-pepper beard—leveled his double-edged axe at the half-orc. "Put the boy down. Slowly."

Kruncher complied. Released from his grip, Kellach rubbed his neck and coughed.

"You lot are all under arrest, by the authority of the watch," the dwarf said. Without a word, the other members of the patrol fanned out and accosted each of the half-orcs. Familiar with the drill, the thugs handed the watchers their weapons and held out their wrists to be tied.

"You're running a bit late tonight, Gwinton," Kellach said to the dwarf when he was able to speak.

"It's just lucky I found you." Gwinton wiped the last of the blood from Driskoll's face and handed Driskoll the handkerchief in case his nose started bleeding again.

"Luck had nothing to do with it," said Kellach. "Your scheduled patrol takes you past this point at five minutes after curfew every night."

"You're a clever lad, for sure," Gwinton said, "but that's not what I meant. You're out after curfew, and you've been brawling to boot. But I'm not going to turn you in to your father."

"That is lucky," said Moyra as she leaped down from her perch atop the doorway.

"No," said Gwinton. "I'm going to take you straight to the magistrate instead."

CHAPTER

3

"I tire of this, children," said Magistrate Lexos.

He looked down at Kellach, Driskoll, and Moyra and shook his head.

The magistrate wore the crimson robe of a cleric of St. Cuthbert, the demigod's insignia embroidered in gold thread across his chest. It struck Driskoll that the symbol—two crossed bars meeting at the center of two circles—looked like an archery target.

Lexos's long, blond hair was tied back into a warrior's braid, although the paunch around his middle indicated that he hadn't hefted a mace since long before Kellach was born. His slightly pointed ears spoke of his elf blood. His pale blue eyes seemed to peer right into the kids' souls.

The magistrate bowed his head for a moment, considering what he was going to say. Driskoll had seen him do this before on the rare mornings that his father hauled him off to hear Lexos preach at the Cathedral of St. Cuthbert. Lexos was preparing to let loose with some fire and brimstone.

"I was performing my sacred duties at the House of the Dead—praying for the departed, paving their way into the afterlife—when I was called in to deal with you boys."

Moyra cleared her throat.

The magistrate looked at Moyra, his chain of thought broken for the moment. He glared at her and said, "Do not worry, young lady—and I use that term loosely. I haven't forgotten about you."

Lexos trained his eyes on Kellach and Driskoll again. "Boys, I can understand how someone like this little miscreant would flaunt the laws of Curston so casually. But I would have thought better of you."

Moyra opened her mouth to protest, but Kellach signaled for her to stay silent.

"As the captain of the watch, your father has enough trouble on his hands, don't you think?" The magistrate waited for a response, but the boys said nothing.

"It's not their fault!"

Lexos and the boys looked at Moyra. She seemed as astonished as they were that those words had leaped from her mouth.

"Kruncher and his friends were chasing me through the square when I ran into these two. They didn't have to help me. It was—" Moyra struggled to find the right word. Then she flashed a smile. "Gallant. Yes, that's it: gallant. Heroic."

Kellach and Driskoll stared at Moyra as if she'd sprouted a second head. It wasn't until Lexos began rumbling again that they thought to turn back around.

"Is this the truth?"

The boys nodded dumbly.

"You think of yourselves as some kind of heroes, eh? Perhaps you've heard the legends of the Knights of the Silver Dragon and aspire to be like them?"

Kellach nodded.

"They were fools!" Lexos said. "You've been told they fought against the evil unleashed by the Sundering, correct? But did you know the Knights caused the Sundering in the first place? That they were responsible for the terrors our city endures every day?"

Moyra and the boys shook their heads.

"Heroes," the magistrate spat. "Let's try this again." He stretched his arms out wide, his palms raised toward the heavens. He spoke a quick prayer to St. Cuthbert for guidance in this trying matter. A warm glow appeared in his cupped hands, swirled about for a moment, and then ran straight up his sleeves and into his ears.

"Now," the magistrate said. "There shall be no lies." He looked at Kellach and Driskoll in turn. "Boys, is what this—is what she says the truth?"

The boys both nodded.

Lexos scowled. "I need to hear you say it."

"Yes," Driskoll blurted. "It's exactly as she said."

"Still," Lexos said, "that doesn't explain what you boys were doing in Main Square after curfew. That's far from your home, isn't it?"

Kellach squirmed under the magistrate's stare. Driskoll had not seen him react that way to anyone since their mother had disappeared.

"I'd rather not get into that," Kellach finally said.

"It's a little late for that," Lexos said. Then, louder he added, "Did Zendric lose his temper with you?"

Kellach's face betrayed nothing, but Driskoll's jaw dropped just a little. "Little happens here that I don't know about," said Lexos.

"You won't tell our father about that, will you?" Driskoll said, then instantly regretted it. Kellach moved to elbow his brother in the ribs, then remembered where they were and thought better of it.

Lexos chuckled softly. "I don't think there's any need for that—as long as you both promise to observe the curfew from now on. It's clear that your service to this 'young lady' outweighs any other transgressions. Isn't it?"

Kellach and Driskoll looked at each other, shocked, then nodded vigorously.

"Good," Lexos said. "I'll save you some trouble and your father some embarrassment. You're free to go. But if you're brought before me again, you'll pay doubly for that infraction and this one too. Understand?"

All three kids nodded this time.

The magistrate turned around and stared out the long, tall window behind his desk. "Excellent," he said as he gazed up at the first stars twinkling overhead. "Gwinton will see you home."

Gwinton led the kids out of the magistrate's office. They walked Moyra home first. As they strode through the thickening dusk, staying close to Gwinton's torch, the watcher asked, "How'd it go with the magistrate?"

The kids scowled at Gwinton. "Hoping he'd throw the book at us?" asked Kellach.

"Sorry about that," Gwinton said, "but you two have been giving your father fits. The watch is under strict orders to bring you before the magistrate if you're found making any trouble."

"Can't he deal with his sons himself?" asked Moyra.

Gwinton shrugged.

"We got off easy," Driskoll said.

Gwinton nodded. "Most of those who violate curfew spend the night in a dank cell. He must like the lot of you."

Kellach shook his head. "I don't think that was it."

Soon, they reached Moyra's home.

"Where have you been?" Moyra's mother, Royma, screeched as she threw open the uneven door to their tiny home. She was dressed in her nightclothes, and her long, gray-streaked hair swept out behind her. Her cruel mouth was ready to launch into one of her tirades, but the sight of the watcher pinched her lips shut.

Fear danced in Royma's dark-gray eyes as she met the watcher's gaze. "Can—can I help you, sir?" she asked.

Gwinton raised his hand to calm the woman's fears. "Your husband is still imprisoned, my lady, at least as far as I know. My business here is not a withdrawal," he said as he gently pushed Moyra forward, "but a deposit."

Royma reached out to Moyra and drew her into the rough, low sitting room behind her. "Go to bed," she said to her daughter, never taking her eyes off the watcher.

Moyra started to protest, but Royma screeched, "Now!"

"My thanks to you, sir," Royma said as Moyra scampered through a doorless portal in the back of the place. The harried woman favored the watcher with a gentle curtsy, then stepped backward and closed the door.

As Gwinton led the boys toward their home, Driskoll asked, "What exactly did Moyra's father do?"

Gwinton laughed. "More like, 'What didn't he do?' That scoundrel was involved in half of the schemes in Curston."

"I know that," Driskoll said, "but what did he get caught doing?"

"Feeding his family," said Kellach, ignoring the harsh look Gwinton flashed him.

Driskoll sighed, exasperated. "Why is it you can never give a straight answer to a straight question?"

"What Breddo did isn't nearly as important as why he did it," Kellach said.

Gwinton and the boys walked the rest of the way home in silence. As they went along, the buildings around them grew progressively newer and nicer. The streets became wider, and eventually lamps lined their edges. The boys lived in the newest part of Curston, known as the Phoenix Quarter, as it had risen from the ashes of the ruins that lay in the southern part of town.

No lights burned in the windows of Torin's home. Driskoll wasn't surprised. Their father was usually occupied with his city watch duties until nearly midnight. Some nights, he was so busy protecting the city that he didn't come home at all.

Gwinton walked Kellach and Driskoll in through the polished green door and waited until they could start a lamp burning.

"I must return to my post," the watcher said.

"Will you see our father?" Driskoll asked.

"I'm sure he already knows." With that, Gwinton snapped a quick salute and left.

The next morning, Driskoll and Kellach woke to find that Torin still wasn't home. The boys wolfed down some bread and cheese, then headed for Zendric's tower.

Curston was just waking up in the gray hour of dawn, and few people walked the streets.

"Are you sure this is a good idea? Zendric seemed pretty angry," Driskoll said.

"This isn't the first time he's kicked me out of the tower," Kellach said. "If I can just talk to him—"

"But he seemed really angry. He might not take you back this time."

Kellach didn't answer.

As the boys neared Zendric's place, Kellach put a hand on Driskoll's chest to stop him in his tracks. "The door's wide open," Kellach said.

"So what?" Driskoll asked. "It's a warm morning."

"Zendric never leaves the door open." Kellach started forward again, more cautiously now. Driskoll followed behind him.

"Maybe one of his potion experiments went bad and he needed to air the place out," Driskoll said.

"This is Zendric. His experiments never go bad."

"There's a first time for everything."

Kellach nodded. "The trick is figuring out what this is the first time for."

Kellach padded up to the edge of the doorway and peered inside. He stood there for a long moment. Driskoll sidled up

21

alongside him and looked inside the place himself.

Not a piece of furniture had been left untoppled. Glass and paper littered the floor, scattered among less identifiable things used by Zendric as ingredients in his potions and spells. Three burning torches lay in the center of it all, their magical flames blazing without heat, leaving the waste on the floor untouched.

Kellach poked Driskoll in the ribs and pointed deep into the room. A heap of robes sprawled along the back wall.

Before Driskoll could ask what they should do, Kellach walked into the place. Crouched low, he made his way to the center of the room and picked up one of the enchanted torches. Driskoll scurried up behind him.

"Are you insane?" Driskoll asked. "We need to call the watch."

"They're too late," Kellach said. "They're only good for chasing off danger. The damage here has already been done."

"Dad might disagree with you."

Kellach shot his brother a disdainful look, then stood up and walked over to the crumpled heap of robes near the back wall. As he went, Driskoll looked about and marveled at the destruction. However it had happened, the people or creatures behind it had one clear objective: to destroy as much of Zendric's home as possible.

A statue of a silver dragon lay in the center of the room. Someone had thrown it to the ground, and it had shattered into dozens of pieces. From inside it, a number of silver pins had fallen out, each bearing the likeness of a dragon rampant, rearing up as if ready to attack.

Driskoll had seen Zendric wear such a pin before, at important affairs. He had thought it unique and possibly priceless. A thief would have stolen such things, but there they lay.

"Zendric!" Driskoll called out loudly.

Kellach shushed him. "You're too late," he said. "He can't hear you."

"You think he's gone?" Driskoll said, peering over Kellach's shoulder as his brother kneeled over the robes on the floor. Then Driskoll realized the robes weren't heaped in a pile. They were still being worn.

Kellach looked up at Driskoll as he rolled Zendric over onto his back. The wizard's eyes were wide open but blank, and a thin line of blood ran out of his mouth and down his cheek.

"No," Kellach said, "I think he's dead."

CHAPTER

4

Driskoll ran screaming out of the front door before Kellach could stop him.

"He's dead," Driskoll shouted. "Murder! Murder!"

Driskoll looked back at the door to Zendric's tower. He almost expected the wizard to come stomping out through it and scold him for disturbing his dreams. Then a horrible thought struck the boy. What if the killer was still inside?

Driskoll looked around for Kellach. His brother hadn't followed him out of the place.

"He's still in there!" Driskoll shouted. He dashed back toward the tower.

When Driskoll reached the door, he stopped at the threshold to peer inside. Kellach held one of the everburning torches in his hand and he stepped carefully along the polished wooden floor. As he went, he waved the torch before him, illuminating every nook and cranny.

The main floor served as a classroom for Zendric's lessons with Kellach and his other occasional students. Worktables and writing desks normally lined the walls of the roughly square chamber. They'd all been turned over, and a few chairs lay in splinters. Unfurled scrolls papered the floor, and fragments of shattered inkpots sat below pitch-colored stains on the fitted-stone walls. Instructional tapestries that had once hung on those walls lay in tatters on the floor. The mantel was bare. Everything that had once stood proudly over the fieldstone fireplace now lay in a jumble to the left.

Kellach scanned the room, his keen eyes taking in everything. He gingerly picked through the debris at the side of the hearth, then nodded to himself and stood.

"What are you looking for?" Driskoll asked. "Shouldn't we get out of here and wait for the watch?"

Kellach shook his head. "They're like minotaurs in a glass-blowing shop. By the time they get through tossing the place, they'll do more damage than whoever killed Zendric."

"It's nothing but a mess," Driskoll said.

"There's more to it than that. This looks like a burglary gone wrong, like Zendric caught some foolish thief in the act of trying to steal from him and was killed for it."

"Could that happen? I mean, this is Zendric, not a shopkeeper."

"I suppose. But it doesn't make sense. There's not much missing. If this was a burglary gone bad, you'd think the burglar would have taken everything not nailed down. There are things worth months of an honest man's wages lying all over the place."

"Maybe the thief got scared after killing Zendric and ran off."

"It's possible, but it's hard to believe that the thief could have made this much of a mess before Zendric was killed. The noise would have woken Zendric up."

Driskoll looked at Zendric's body. "How long do you think he's been gone?" he asked.

"His body's still warm."

"I've never seen a dead body before."

Kellach moved back by the corpse and kneeled down to inspect it. "The strange thing, though, is I can't see what killed him. There's not a mark on him."

"What about the blood on his mouth?"

"Okay, his lip is split, probably from when he hit the floor by the looks of it. But that's it. There aren't any other wounds on him, and a busted lip isn't fatal."

Kellach stood up. "Maybe this was supposed to look like an accident. Zendric had a lot of enemies, you know. No one gets to be that powerful without making someone angry—or at least jealous."

Driskoll swallowed hard. "Someone killed Zendric on purpose?"

"Possibly."

"So what do you think happened?"

Kellach thought about it for a moment, rubbing his still-beardless chin. Then he said three words rarely spoken from his mouth: "I don't know."

Driskoll let his jaw drop. "You don't have any idea?"

Kellach shook his head. "No, no, no. I have lots of ideas. Too many of them, in fact. I don't know which one might be right."

Kellach headed for the polished wooden stairs at the room's back wall. At the top of the stairs, another ironbound door stood ajar.

"Where are you going?" Driskoll asked.

"To have a look around. Come on," Kellach said, his hand already on the railing. A long, wooden snake spiraled around the entire length of the handrail. The post cap at the bottom was a massive snake's ruby-eyed head, fangs extended. It looked ready to sink into the arm of anyone foolish enough to traverse the stairs without permission.

"Are you sure we should go up there?" Driskoll asked.

"We don't have much time. Thanks to you, the watch will be here any moment."

With that, Kellach raced up the stairs and disappeared. Driskoll stared after his brother for a moment, then he looked down with a start. He was standing next to Zendric's body— his *dead* body. Driskoll launched himself up the stairs without a backward glance, taking care to not touch the railing as he went.

The tower's second floor housed Zendric's private workspace. The ceiling here was slightly higher than that on the first level. Morning light streamed in through the tall windows. A midnight-blue carpet embroidered with the paths of planets and stars covered most of the polished floorboards.

Shelves overflowing with thick, leather-bound books filled one wall. A neatly arranged array of vellum scrolls occupied the other. Three overstuffed leather chairs stood near the hearth. Near the windows overlooking the street sat a large, oak writing desk. A gold-trimmed spellbook lay open upon it, surrounded by loose notes and drawings. Several everburning torches lit the space, including one right above the desk. The room smelled of must, the same smell that Driskoll associated with libraries and knowledge.

Kellach leaned over Zendric's desk and inspected the spell-book as Driskoll padded up behind him. The book was so fat that Driskoll doubted he could have carried it without Kellach's help. The words and diagrams on the open page were written in an exacting hand and in several colors of ink, but Driskoll couldn't understand a bit of them.

"He was in the middle of copying a spell," said Kellach, not bothering to turn around. "He must not have been expecting company. He left off in the middle of a word." Kellach pointed to the sleek, white-feathered quill resting at the bottom of the page. The ink on its tip was red, and it was still wet.

"Shouldn't that have dried by now?" Driskoll asked.

Kellach shook his head. "It's an everwet quill," he said. "Self-inking. It never runs dry."

"I don't think this was a robbery," said Driskoll. "A thief would have made his way up here. That collection of scrolls must be worth a fortune."

Kellach nodded. "Maybe Zendric wasn't supposed to be here."

"Did he have plans for last night?"

"He didn't tell me everything he did." Kellach hesitated for a moment. "But I did notice one thing missing."

Driskoll waited.

"You remember that glass ball I was holding yesterday when Zendric lost his temper?" Kellach said.

"The one with the gold bands around it?" Driskoll asked.

"I couldn't find that anywhere. It was always on the mantel. Zendric never would tell me what it was."

"So why were you messing with it?"

"Because it was off-limits." Kellach shrugged.

"Maybe it got knocked into a corner."

Kellach shook his head. "I looked almost everywhere. It's not here."

"Maybe the killer was after the globe?" Driskoll said.

"So the killer came in to take the globe, and Zendric caught him." Kellach looked thoughtful.

"Right. Then he kills Zendric, grabs the globe, and tears the place apart to cover the theft."

Kellach nodded. "It's plausible enough."

As Kellach continued poking through the papers on Zendric's desk, Driskoll glanced out through the window. He could see over many of the tops of the low buildings across the street and beyond.

The morning sun shone down on Curston, brightening the slanting, shale-shingled roofs. The light glinted in the dew. Washing flapped from clotheslines strung between the dormer windows of the houses across the way.

Two sparrows chirped from the roof across the street.

It looks so peaceful, Driskoll thought.

Then a high-pitched voice stabbed above the sound of the birds. Driskoll looked down to see a woman scurrying up the street toward the tower, followed by a squad of blue-uniformed watchers. It was her voice that pierced the dawn air.

She pointed at Zendric's home. "I heard the boy say 'Murder!' "

The watchers parted like a herd of sheep before a horseman as one man stepped forward. Driskoll gasped.

"What is it?" Kellach said.

"Dad."

Kellach scowled. "He's getting faster." He nudged his brother aside from Zendric's desk. "Go down and stall him."

"Are you kidding? I'm not going to face down a full squad of watchers."

Kellach started shuffling through the material scattered on the desk. "I might find something in Zendric's papers to explain all this, but I need more time." He turned to his little brother. "It's your fault they're here. Do something about it."

"Not on your life."

Kellach glared at his brother. "We don't have time to argue about this. Do it. Now!"

Driskoll hesitated for a moment. He looked into his brother's eyes. Kellach was as serious as Driskoll had ever seen him.

Driskoll sprinted down the stairs and out the front door. As he reached the street, the sunlight blinded him. He blinked as he looked around for his father, but he didn't see him. For a moment, he hoped the woman had led the watchers away toward someone else's murder.

Then a hand fell on Driskoll's shoulder, and a familiar voice spoke in his ear.

"Suppose you tell me, Drisk, just what's going on?" He turned to see his father, Torin, standing there in his watcher's uniform. He threw himself into Torin's arms.

"We got here in time for Kellach's lesson, just like always, but the door was wide open, and Zendric looked dead. That's when I ran out here into the street shouting 'murder.'" Driskoll pulled back, avoiding his father's steely eyes. "It was all just a mistake though. It turned out Zendric was just sleeping." He tried to force a laugh, but it came out feeble and hollow.

Torin gave Driskoll a quick embrace, then put his hands on Driskoll's shoulders. "That's not very funny," Torin said. "Are you all right?"

Driskoll bowed his head and nodded slowly. "Just a little shook up, I guess."

Torin reached down and pulled Driskoll's chin up so he could look into his son's eyes. "You're sure about this?" Driskoll twisted his head to avoid his father's gaze. But Torin arched his neck around until he could look directly into his son's eyes.

Torin shook his head. "You're a terrible liar, Drisk. Tell me what really happened." Torin's eyes narrowed. "Is Zendric really dead?"

Driskoll nodded.

Torin turned and barked at a watcher named Kalmbur. "Get the magistrate," he said. "Now!" Kalmbur dashed off for Lexos's offices.

"The rest of you, surround the tower," Torin said to the remaining watchers. "Under no circumstances should you enter the building. Wait until I give the word."

As the watchers scrambled to get into position around the tower, Torin and Driskoll stood together and watched the door. More and more watchers arrived to lend aid. The news of the trouble at Zendric's tower had spread like a raging fire leaping the city's rooftops.

"You three," Torin said, motioning to the first squad of watchers, "block off the north end of the street. You three, take the south. The rest of you clear the street. This could get ugly fast."

Torin spun around to greet another group of watchers. "You lot stand with me, and get out your swords. We have no idea—"

Torin cut himself short. "Wait a minute. Where's your brother?"

Driskoll glanced up at the tower's second floor window, then shrugged. "I think he went home."

Torin scowled at his son. "You really are a rotten liar."

Torin turned to the watchers assembled about him. "Wait here," he said, "and make sure this one doesn't go anywhere."

Torin drew his sword and charged into the tower through the open door.

Driskoll waited. He soon realized he was holding his breath, but he was too tense to let it loose.

Just when Driskoll thought he might burst, a howl issued from the tower's second floor. A few moments later, Torin stormed out of Zendric's tower, holding Kellach's ear and marching his elder son before him.

"Ow! Ow, ow, ow, ow, ow!" Kellach yelped.

Torin pushed Kellach across the street by his ear and deposited him next to Driskoll. As Kellach rubbed his ear, Torin launched into a tirade that turned Driskoll's ears as red as Kellach's.

"What were you thinking? This is a crime scene! Don't you ever, *ever* . . ."

Driskoll couldn't bear to listen anymore. He covered his ears and peeked down the street. The other watchers had marched off to reinforce the cordons at both ends of the block. Behind the blockades, a few of Zendric's neighbors protested, telling the watchers that they needed to get to their homes, but no one was let through.

Of all the watchers, only Gwinton was brave enough to glance at the boys. When the dwarf caught Driskoll looking at him, he just shook his head.

As Torin was in the middle of describing how the world would end in flames before he let the boys out of the house again, Kalmbur arrived with the magistrate in tow.

Kalmbur tapped him on the shoulder.

Torin turned around. "How many times do I have to tell you! Don't interrupt me when—" Torin took one look at the magistrate, and the words caught in his throat. Lexos ignored what he had heard of Torin's colorful language and got straight to the point.

"What's happened here, Captain?"

Torin collected himself. "Zendric is apparently dead, sir."

Lexos arched his eyebrows. "Apparently? Have you seen a corpse?"

Torin shook his head. "Only briefly. We were waiting for you to arrive when I learned that my eldest was still in the tower. I extracted him immediately and then returned to await your orders."

"Is your son unharmed?"

"So far, sir."

Lexos allowed himself a ghost of a smile.

"See that he stays that way." He turned his attention toward the tower's open door.

"Now that I'm here," said Lexos, "let's see what there is to see." With that, he walked across the street and through Zendric's door.

"You boys stay here," Torin said, and then he disappeared into the tower. Two full squads of watchers followed behind, all with their blades at the ready. Kellach grabbed Driskoll by the arm and pulled him after them.

33

When the boys entered the tower, they found the mess was already much worse. The watchers were busy tearing through the place, looking for any sort of person or creature that might have murdered a wizard.

"Have some care!" Torin bellowed. "If Zendric is returned to us, he is sure to skin those watchers who destroy his property." The frequency of the crashes dropped but did not halt.

Lexos stood at the hearth, his back to the boys, as if he was composing himself. He turned around and spotted the boys looking at him. For a moment, it seemed he might have Torin banish them from the tower, but instead he nodded at them with a dour grimace. Then he walked over to the wizard's corpse and dropped to his knees next to it.

The priest closed his eyes as he chanted and raised his arms toward the sky. A soft, golden glow enveloped both him and the wizard's body. Torin stood over the magistrate, waiting patiently.

Driskoll was in awe. Even though he'd spent many long hours watching Kellach practice his spells, divine magic like this was something else.

While wizards like Kellach tapped into the basic energies of the world to forge their magic, clerics like Lexos worked their spells by asking for favors directly from their chosen gods. The glow meant that Driskoll was in the presence of the divine, perhaps St. Cuthbert himself. It was all he could do not to drop straight to his knees. The only thing stopping him was the fear of interrupting Lexos in his prayers.

After a moment, however, the glow flickered out like a candle guttering in a stiff breeze. To Driskoll, its loss felt like the sun slipping back behind a cloud, maybe forever.

"What's wrong?" Torin asked, breaking the silence. "Can you not help him?"

Lexos stood up and regarded Torin. "It's as I feared," he said. "Zendric is not truly dead."

"Why is that a bad thing?" Driskoll whispered.

Kellach motioned for him to shush.

It was too late. Lexos waved them forward. "Come, my sons, you who discovered this terrifying tableau. You deserve to hear the rest."

Kellach and Driskoll shuffled forward under Torin's withering glare. Finding a wizard's body was one thing. Delaying the investigation had been even worse. Ignoring his order to stay outside topped them all.

Still, Torin held his tongue as Lexos spoke. "As amazing as it might seem, Zendric is not dead. His fate is far worse."

"What could be worse than death?" Driskoll asked.

Lexos chuckled. "I forget how young you lads are. I pray you never discover the myriad destinies that hold worse fears than mortality. Our friend Zendric has fallen to one of these. His body may be alive—for now—but his spirit has fled!"

CHAPTER

5

The room fell into a stunned silence. For a long moment, no one could think of a thing to say. Finally, Torin spoke.

"You say 'his spirit has fled'? Exactly what does that mean?"

Lexos cleared his throat. "You are aware that all mindful creatures are given a soul at the moment of their creation?"

Torin nodded. "I do attend your services."

"From time to time," Lexos said with a soft snort. "In any case—or, at least, in most cases—the soul stays with the owner's earthly shell throughout its life. When the shell dies, the soul usually remains in the area for a while."

Lexos paused and looked around the room. Everyone in the room was hanging on his every word.

Satisfied, Lexos continued. "If Zendric had been killed by normal means, I would expect to find his soul lingering about for a bit, perhaps several days. Even if he had passed on to his greater reward, I would normally be able to contact his soul in its new home, by the grace of St. Cuthbert.

"However, all my efforts have met with utter and abject failure. I have made the proper prayers and offered up the correct blessings to St. Cuthbert, but to no end. As best as I can tell, our good friend Zendric's soul has simply disappeared."

The others in the room remained silent for a moment as they tried to digest what Lexos had said. It was Kellach who spoke first.

"Can't you call him back?"

Torin reached over and put a rough hand on Kellach's shoulder. Fire burned in his eyes. "I'll not have a son of mine speak so openly to the magistrate about such matters. You forget your place too readily."

Lexos put up a hand to stay Torin's wrath. "Forgive the lad," he said. "We may have a murder on our hands, but your son has lost both a teacher and a friend."

"I intended no offense, sir," said Kellach. He looked straight at the magistrate.

"And none was taken," said Lexos. "You asked a fine question, and I am happy to provide a sharp, young mind like yours with an answer.

"All I can say for certain is that Zendric's soul is not available to me. I can only conjecture at the reasons. It may have been destroyed. It may have simply fled beyond my ability to track it down."

"If it is fled?" Kellach asked.

"Then it may be recovered," Lexos said. "If we could manage to contact Zendric's soul, wherever it may be, then I could call upon the powers of St. Cuthbert to return one of Curston's finest citizens to us."

"You have such powers over life and death?" Kellach asked.

Lexos chuckled. "Not I, lad. St. Cuthbert. I am only a channel for his will. If he deemed Zendric worthy, then we could have him back among us once again. And I would argue my old friend's case strongly. But even St. Cuthbert cannot recreate a missing soul. Some things are beyond even the gods."

"If you have such powers, where were you when our mother vanished?" Driskoll blurted, surprising even himself. The tears running down his heated cheeks seemed to have sprung from nowhere.

"That's enough!" Torin snapped. He grabbed Driskoll by the arm and hauled him into the street. Kellach offered a quick apology to Lexos on Driskoll's behalf before following the rest of his family out of the tower.

Torin dragged Driskoll along until he reached the nearest empty doorway. He thrust his younger son up against the doorframe, partially shielding him from the prying eyes of the watchers at the nearest streetcorners.

"What in the name of the gods has gotten into that head of yours, Driskoll?" Torin said between clenched teeth, his nose only inches from his son's.

Driskoll brushed at the few, fat tears still rolling down his cheeks and silently shook his head.

Torin leaned in closer, his index finger right in Driskoll's face. "Your mother has been gone for over five years. You're no longer a little boy. It's time you grew up! There can be no excuses for what you just did in there."

Driskoll couldn't think of a thing to say. He just nodded and nodded.

"Dad," said Kellach, who was standing behind Torin, just out of arm's reach. Torin wheeled on him, pointing his finger at Kellach now, about to launch into another, related tirade.

"They need you back in the tower," Kellach said, glancing at the watchers standing guard at both ends of the street.

Torin cursed, then said to Kellach, "Take him home. Now. I don't want to see either of you for the rest of the day."

Kellach nodded. "Yes, sir."

Torin stormed back toward the tower without looking back.

Kellach came over and put his arm around Driskoll's shoulder. Looking down at his little brother, he said, "You heard the man. Let's go."

Driskoll started to apologize, but he choked on the words.

Kellach shook his head as they walked along. He was silent until they were well past the watchers and the gawkers at the end of the block. Then he spoke.

"It's not your fault," Kellach told Driskoll. "The same question popped into my head."

"Why didn't you ask it?" Driskoll used both hands to wipe his face dry. His cheeks still burned hot, but he was starting to recover.

"Because I knew the answer. Or at least the one that Lexos had ready for us."

Driskoll kept walking, waiting for Kellach to continue.

"The gods only have so much time for mortals. It's up to priests like Lexos to guide them in how to spend their divine energies, mostly through devout prayer. The more powerful the priest, the more their chosen god listens to their pleas.

"Mom wasn't the only person who went missing after the seal was sundered. Curston lost a lot of people."

Driskoll nodded. He knew that even all the clerics in Curston couldn't have saved everyone lost in the attack that had claimed his mother. In his head, it made sense. But his heart wasn't listening to reason.

"Who did get saved that day?" Driskoll asked.

Kellach shook his head. "A handful of the most important people in the city. I'm not positive about everyone. The only one I know about for sure was Dad."

"Why not Mom too?"

"She wasn't important enough, it seems."

Driskoll started choking up again. "She was important enough to me!"

As the brothers kept walking, getting closer to their home, Kellach hugged Driskoll with the arm he still had around him. "Me too. But we don't get to make these decisions. They leave that to the rich and powerful in town."

Driskoll thought about it for a moment. "Then I want to be rich and powerful someday."

Kellach nodded. "Why do you think I'm studying with Zendric?"

Driskoll looked up at Kellach to see him grinning. Driskoll had to laugh.

As the boys turned down the last corner before reaching their home, a voice rang out. "There you two are! I've been looking all over for you."

Moyra leaped down from the windowsill on the front of the boys' house. She dashed over to Kellach and Driskoll and looked them each in the eye. Driskoll was sure she could tell he'd been crying.

"I suppose you already know about Zendric," Moyra said.

"We found him," Kellach said. Driskoll nodded in agreement, not wishing to speak for fear that his voice would betray him again.

Moyra's face pinched in sympathy. "I'm so sorry," she said.

"There's nothing to be sorry about," Kellach said, "yet."

"What do you mean?" said Moyra. "I heard Zendric was dead."

"It seems that Zendric's soul has fled." Driskoll's voice was raw, but he made a point of speaking clearly.

"Isn't that the same thing?" Moyra asked.

"It might be," Kellach explained, "and it might not. It depends on what happened to his soul. If some demon devoured it, then it might be gone forever. Or it may have been stolen and put away someplace. At the moment, I don't have enough information to tell."

Moyra looked at Kellach hard. "Are you telling me that your teacher was trucking with demons?"

Kellach put up his hands. "Not at all! But he made many enemies over the years. Why, in the time after the Sundering of the Seal alone he must have banished dozens of demons and devils himself—or so I hear. Any one of them might have had a friend waiting for the proper time to exact revenge."

"But why now?" Moyra asked. "It's been years since the Sundering."

"You're asking me to fathom the mind of a demon?" Kellach asked. "You might as well ask me to pluck Zendric's soul from my pocket."

"Well, you are a wizard, aren't you? Maybe you can do something to get back his soul."

"Like what? Zendric is always telling me I'm not ready for anything but simple spells."

"Well, he's not around now to do that, is he?" said Moyra. "We have to do something. And I think I know where we can start." Defiance sparkled in her emerald eyes.

Kellach rubbed his chin. "In a sense, we're Zendric's only hope."

"What?" It was all Driskoll could manage.

Kellach waved back in the direction of Zendric's tower. "You know how Dad and the watch will handle this. They'll round up all the murderers and thieves they can find and subject them all to various trials that won't mean a thing."

"They'll dunk them in one of the wells," Moyra said, a self-satisfied look on her face. "That's what they did to my dad. He got so much water into him he had to confess to that burglary, even though he didn't do it."

"How do you know that?" Driskoll asked.

"He told me so!"

"And you believed him? He's one of the most notorious thieves in all of Curston!"

Moyra stepped right up into Driskoll's face and started shouting. "He's my dad! He wouldn't lie to me! In fact, if it hadn't been for your father, he wouldn't be rotting in that prison right now!"

Driskoll brought up his arms to shove Moyra back, but Kellach reached in and pulled them apart. "That's enough!" he said. He sounded just like Torin at that moment, and Driskoll hated him for it.

Moyra and Driskoll turned their backs to each other. "This is exactly why I haven't come around here since then," she said. "I knew you'd take his side!"

"He's our father!" Driskoll said.

Kellach reached up and grabbed both Driskoll and Moyra's ears and pulled hard. "Grow up!" he said.

"Now listen," Kellach said to the two younger kids in a low, dangerous voice. "If we're going to find out what happened to Zendric, we need to put an end to this bickering."

"We can handle it without her," Driskoll said. In fact, he had no idea if he and Kellach could handle it with the entire city behind them. But that didn't quell his anger. "What did she come around here for anyway?"

"Wouldn't you like to know," Moyra said, folding her arms in front of her.

"Actually," Kellach said, "that's a fine question. Now, what was your idea, Moyra?"

"You don't care," Moyra said.

Kellach shoved a finger in Driskoll's face before he could respond. "I certainly do," he said to her. "I'm also curious as to how you already knew about Zendric. Even in Curston, news rarely travels that fast."

"That's what I came to tell you," said Moyra, unfolding her arms. "I was visiting my dad this morning, and he asked whether I'd heard anything about Zendric."

"Why?" Driskoll asked. He realized he wasn't angry anymore. This was too important.

"That's what I asked him. 'No reason, love,' he says. 'I just heard some talk going 'round the circuit here is all.'

"I didn't think much of it at the time. But on my way back home from the prison, I thought I'd stop by and mention it to Zendric. When I got to the end of his street, the watchers were there standing guard. I tried to tell them that I knew your dad and needed to talk to him, but they wouldn't hear it, so I came back here."

Kellach nodded for a moment, then said, "You must take us to see your father."

"No!" Driskoll said. "I mean, why? Moyra just told us everything her dad said. You heard it."

Kellach grimaced. "That's exactly why we must visit him in prison. I need to know more."

"He's only allowed one visitor per day," Driskoll said. "Blood relatives only. We don't qualify."

"We'll just have to find a way around that rule. We must speak to him," Kellach said. It wasn't a plea but a statement of fact.

Driskoll stopped shaking his head, but remained defiant. "Let Moyra go talk with him tomorrow."

"There's no time," Kellach said. "We have to find out what happened to Zendric. If we can find Zendric's soul and return it to his body, we might be able to save him. But if we wait," Kellach took a quick breath, "he may be lost to us forever."

Driskoll squinted at Kellach for a moment, then looked over at Moyra, who nodded at him. "All right," he said finally. "Let's go."

CHAPTER

6

Curston's prison sat under the Watchers' Hall. The prison was built soon after the city was founded, back when it was still named Promise. Being mostly underground, the prison survived the Sundering of the Seal as well as dozens of other disasters over the centuries.

The Watchers' Hall above hadn't always been so fortunate, having been rebuilt at least three different times. The last time was right after the Sundering. The Watchers' Hall had burned to the ground, cooking the occupants of the prison's upper level but leaving those in the darker regions unscathed.

Sadly—according to Torin, at least—the people in the lower depths were the worst of the lot. "Much good would have been done if the smoke from that fire had reached a bit lower that day," Driskoll often heard him say.

The new Watchers' Hall stretched atop the prison on the edge of Broken Town. It was said that a watcher standing on the very tip of the hall's front tower could see into every alley in Broken Town. It took so long, however, to get down from the place that by the time a watcher was able to report a crime in progress, it was too late to do anything about it.

Never one to let such a problem stop him, Torin instituted a system in which a pair of watchers stood on the tower's roof around the clock. Whenever they saw something suspicious, they wrote a note about it. They stuffed the note into a hollow wooden ball the size of a man's fist and dropped the ball down the tower's stairwell.

The balls sometimes landed on visitors or rookie watchers walking past. The veterans would laugh and say, "I guess he needed a good smack on the head."

Kellach, Moyra, and Driskoll walked into the Watchers' Hall like they owned the place, striding straight through the tower's base, past the tower stairway, and into the building proper. Kellach and Driskoll had been welcome there since each of them was able to walk. Moyra was happy to follow their lead.

"Welcome, boys!" Sergeant Guffy said as the kids strolled in through the front door. Guffy was a kind old man who had lost the leg to a werewolf in the weeks after the Sundering. He'd been stationed behind the duty desk in the foyer ever since. "I'm afraid your father's not here. Out on some nasty business involving—" Guffy glanced at Kellach.

"Well, I suppose he'll tell you all about it himself later," the sergeant finished. "What can I do for you lads—and you too, darling." He looked Moyra up and down, his wide and easy smile never faltering.

"We're here to see my father," Moyra said.

"Ah, I see," said Guffy. "I was afraid of that, darling. You know the rules. Only one visit per person per day."

Moyra began to protest, but Kellach cut her off. "*We're* here to see her father," he told Guffy. "She's here as our guest."

Guffy grimaced. "I'm sorry, lad. Much as I'd like to bend the rules for you, your father would have my head."

"But it's important!" said Driskoll, his voice cracking.

"I don't doubt it," said Guffy, "but so are the rules. I don't make them, and I don't break them. Not even for you."

When Guffy noticed how badly the three kids were taking the news, he added, "Of course, lads, there's one easy way around all this."

"What's that?" asked Driskoll, his face brightening.

"Just get your father to come down here with you."

The kids' faces all fell again.

"Thanks, Guffy," Kellach said as he herded Driskoll and Moyra toward the door. "We'll be back."

"Now what?" Driskoll asked as the three left the Watchers' Hall. "We wait until tomorrow?"

"We don't have time," said Kellach.

"Maybe we should get Dad."

"This is exactly the kind of thing he doesn't want us doing." Kellach shook his head. "We'll have to sneak in."

"You're insane!" said Driskoll. "Smart people try to break out of prison, not in."

"It's not as hard as it sounds," said Moyra. "The prison is set up to keep people in, not out. We're not trying to open a cell door, just talk through it."

"So all we have to do," Driskoll said, "is get past Guffy."

"I have an idea," said Kellach, "but it's going to take someone with fast hands."

Moyra smiled. "I'm your girl."

Kellach pulled out his spellbook and an everwet quill from his robes and scribbled something down on a blank sheet. He tore the sheet from the book, folded it small enough to fit inside a fist, and handed it to Moyra. "Take this into the tower's stairwell. Catch the next ball that drops down and stuff this into it, along with the note that's already there."

"Where are you going to be?"

"Once you place the note, hand it to a watcher. Then hustle over to Guffy's desk. We'll meet you there."

Driskoll and Kellach walked into the building. Moyra waited a moment before following them.

Inside the stairwell, Moyra spotted a handful of hollow wooden balls scattered about the place. Above her, the narrow stairway spiraled up through the tower's stone interior. Sunlight stabbed through the tall, thin windows that appeared regularly along the stairway. The stairs stopped at the watchers' observation platform several dozen feet over her head.

Moyra braced herself to dodge the next ball falling from above. But nothing happened. After a couple of minutes, she grew anxious. She could be there for hours waiting for a ball to drop. She tiptoed over to where one of the empty balls lay. Making sure no one was watching, she snatched it up and stuffed Kellach's note into it. Then she threw the ball up into the air and ducked out of the stairwell before it landed.

As soon as the ball smacked into the ground, a watcher strode into the stairwell. He picked up the ball, pulled out the note, and read it. Then he swore and dashed off.

Moyra followed him, whistling a happy tune.

48

Meanwhile, the boys had found Guffy still sitting behind his desk.

"Back again so soon, lads?" asked Guffy. "You can't sweet-talk me."

"Wouldn't think of it," said Kellach. "We just thought we'd catch up a bit. We don't see you much anymore."

Guffy smiled. The boys chatted with him for a moment before the watcher came running up to Guffy with Moyra right behind him. He held a sheet of unfolded vellum in his hand. "You'll want to see this," the watcher said.

Annoyed at being interrupted, Guffy snatched the note from the watcher and read it, his lips moving as he scanned the page. "So there's a house on fire, Fasken? Go put it out."

"Did you see the address?" Fasken said.

"Corner of Central and—that's my place!" Snatching up his crutch, Guffy leaped from behind his desk and hobbled off, the younger watcher right behind him. They nearly knocked over Moyra as they left.

"No time now, dear," Guffy said. "I'll send someone back to deal with you in a moment."

Kellach waited until the two watchers were out of sight, then turned to the thick, ironbound door behind Guffy's desk.

"Quickly," he said as he pulled the door open. Moyra and Driskoll dashed over the threshold.

"Follow me," Moyra said, and she led her friends down into the prison.

The stone of the prison's walls was a dark gray, nearly black, but the place was well lit, with smokeless torches burning in regularly spaced sconces. The ceiling was low, but the halls were wide enough that people could walk down them in a single file without being able to touch the walls on either side, no matter how far they stretched their arms.

The smell in the place was awful. Many people lived in this large warren, and few of them were clean. Many a chamber pot had been spilled—or thrown—with little ever done to clean up the mess.

As the trio walked down the main hall, arms reached out of the grates in some of the ironbound doorways. Some of the voices behind those doors screamed for help. Others cursed the three as they passed. All were desperate, and none were friendly.

Kellach and Driskoll followed Moyra around a number of turns before she finally came to a halt. She stood before a door that looked much like any of the others, and she beat on it.

"What in the name of the cursed gods do you want?" a voice said from beyond the grating. "I'm not due for my daily beating until after sundown, you tin-bladed buffoon."

"You have guests," Driskoll said.

"I've already seen the only guest I care for today," the voice said.

"Daddy!" Moyra blurted out. "It's me!"

The man inside the cell slipped as he scrambled to his feet, but he still reached the door in an instant. He was short enough that he had to stand on his toes to see through the upper grate. "Baby, it is you!" he shouted.

Breddo fell to his knees and looked out at the trio through the lower grating, one normally used by dwarves, halflings, and gnomes. Moyra kneeled down and hugged her father through the iron bars.

Before his arrest, Moyra's father had been the most charming person in Broken Town—and perhaps all of Curston. Though the prison had coated him with a layer of filth that might never come off, the light inside of him still remained undimmed. Even on his knees behind a prison door, he radiated confidence. Driskoll was amazed the guards didn't simply hand over his cell's key to him when asked.

"Thank you, lads!" Breddo said. "I don't know how you managed to arrange for another visit today from my most precious daughter. But you can rest assured this is one favor I shall never forget."

Kellach spoke. "I beg your pardon, sir, but we don't have much time."

Breddo looked at Kellach closely and narrowed his eyes at him. "You're down here without permission."

Kellach nodded. Before he could speak, a door slammed somewhere in the distance, followed by the sound of boots marching down a long set of stairs. "Moyra told us you asked her about Zendric this morning."

Breddo smiled and wagged his finger at Kellach. "And good student that you are, you're here to learn more, right? Clever boy. No use feeding rumors to a wizard. But wait!"

Breddo pressed his face against the bars that separated them. As he stared into Kellach's eyes, a frown spread across his lips. "We're too late, aren't we?"

The thief dropped back onto his rump. He sat on the floor of his cell, which was covered with moldering hay. He hid his face in his hands.

"Not quite, Daddy," Moyra said, a bit of hope in her voice. She quickly filled him in.

Breddo nodded in amazement throughout his daughter's account, then spoke.

"Yesterday evening, just after dusk, the watchers brought in a group of young thugs. One of them was already wanted for thievery. He was to spend a full year in our grand company.

"As you boys probably know, a thief can have the remainder of his sentence commuted if he agrees to give up something most precious to him: a hand. Since most thieves know life is hard enough already without being maimed, few accept the offer.

"But this lad didn't hesitate. From what I'm told, he put his hand up readily enough. Once the operation was complete, his wound was bandaged, and he was sent on his merry way."

"What does this have to do with Zendric?" Driskoll asked. He glanced up and down the hallway. A watcher might find them any second.

"Patience, lad," Breddo grinned. "I'm getting to that.

"While this thief went free, his friends still had to spend the night. Like most bullies, they were a mouthy lot. They told those nearby that their leader wouldn't be down for long. They said he had a job to do that night that would make up for everything. All he had to do was break into the home of the most powerful wizard in town."

"Zendric!" said Driskoll.

Breddo nodded. "I didn't think much of it at the time, just pointless bragging by bullies who were hoping to scare the rest of us. But when Moyra came by this morning, I felt compelled to mention it to her."

Breddo looked up at Kellach. "Perhaps I was thinking of you, my boy. Moyra tells me you're Zendric's best student. I suppose I didn't want any harm coming to him for that reason at least."

"Thanks," said Kellach, "I think. Can you tell us anything else? Are the braggarts still here?"

Breddo shook his head. "They were released this morning. Since they were only charged with breaking curfew, Lexos apparently didn't feel the need to extend their visit with us. They made no friends on the way out, though, I can tell you. Spitting into every cell as they passed. When they end up back here—and I can guarantee that sort will—they'll find an even chillier reception awaiting them."

Driskoll heard footsteps clomping down the hallway toward Breddo's cell.

Breddo smiled. "I think, children, our visit is almost at an end. What else can I tell you?"

"Do you know how we might find them? Who were they?" Kellach said, desperation creeping into his voice.

"I never saw them, my boy," Breddo said. "But I did hear the young ones mention their friend's name loudly, several times over."

"And? Who was it?"

"His name was—"

"Hold it right there!" From the end of the corridor, Guffy came stumping after the three friends.

"Run!" Moyra shouted. The trio sprinted away as fast as their legs could carry them. Guffy sent up a shout, and the sound of more sets of boots joined the pursuit.

Moyra led the boys through the maze of low halls like they were her home. At first, she headed away from the prison entrance, drawing the watchers deeper into the heart of the place. Then, she led the boys back around, racing up a parallel set of halls.

"If we circle around to the door quickly, we can escape before they think to cut us off," she panted.

Snapping a signal with her hand, Moyra brought the boys to a sharp halt. She peered around a nearby corner.

"All clear." She beckoned for the boys to follow her.

All that now stood between the friends and the stairs up into the Watchers' Hall was a single hallway lined with cells. They nearly started laughing as they sped toward the end of the hall.

But just as they passed the final cell, Guffy limped out of a side passage. He stood in front of the stairwell.

"I knew you'd try this!" he said.

Moyra turned to run in the opposite direction, but the echoes of boots sounded out behind them. There was no escape. The trio slowly backed away.

"Breaking into the jail is a serious offense," Guffy said as he came closer. "I doubt your father will—"

A hairy gray arm darted out from a cell and grabbed Guffy by the throat. He yelped in surprise and dropped his crutch. All three kids jumped. For a moment, they watched as the arm reeled Guffy in closer. Then Driskoll shoved Moyra and Kellach from behind.

"We have to help him!" he shouted.

Driskoll and Moyra jumped forward and clawed at the prisoner's arm. Kellach picked up Guffy's crutch and stabbed the end of it through the bars in the cell's door. The prisoner yelped as the tip smashed into his nose.

Guffy fell to the ground, clutching his throat and gasping for breath. "If you kids think this means I owe you anything," he rasped, "then you'd better keep running."

The kids stared at Guffy.

"What are you waiting for?" the prisoner snarled from behind his cell door. "Take a hint. Go!"

The trio dashed past Guffy. As they leaped up the stairs, they heard Breddo's voice shouting after them. They couldn't make out the words, but the other prisoners took up the message, passing it along as quickly as they could. By the time the kids reached the prison's door, the words had become a chant. As Moyra, Driskoll, and Kellach sprang through the door toward freedom, the voices of dozens of prisoners sang in their ears.

"Kruncher! Kruncher! His name was Kruncher!"

CHAPTER

7

It was all that Kellach, Moyra, and Driskoll could do to contain themselves until they left Guffy and Watchers' Hall far behind. Moyra was the first to break.

"Kruncher!" she nearly yelled. "Can you believe it?"

Kellach shook his head.

"What now?" Driskoll asked.

"We track him down and find out what happened," Kellach said.

"I know just the place," said Moyra. "Broken Town, here we come!"

Driskoll stopped walking. "Are you sure that's a good idea?"

Kellach grimaced. "I don't see that we have any other choice."

"Why don't we just tell Dad?"

"To find him, we'd have to ask a watcher, and they're not too happy with us right now. Neither is he. We might spend the whole day in prison before he comes to check up on us."

"Don't worry, Driskoll," Moyra said. "It might be the roughest part of town, but it's like home to me." Moyra sauntered off. The boys scrambled to keep up with her.

As Moyra led the way through the shattered streets, they passed a local kid leaning against a building and picking his teeth with a knife. When he spotted the strangers, he swaggered forward to intercept them.

Moyra shot the filth-covered thug a murderous look. He stopped in his tracks and turned his attention back to cleaning his teeth.

Eventually, the trio reached the darkest street of them all. Even now, just before noon, the buildings on either side of the street reached up to choke out the light. Down below, at the foot of the gloom, there stood a seedy tavern. The wooden sign above the doorway bore a painting of a hairless panther. The sign squeaked as it swung on its rusty chain.

"Here it is," Moyra said. "The Skinned Cat."

"Gods," Driskoll said. "How did it get a name like that?"

Moyra looked back at him. "Trust me. You don't want to know."

The rough-hewn door sprang open, and a halfling flew out and landed in a heap on the broken cobblestones before them. He didn't move.

"Is he—" Driskoll gulped.

Moyra wrinkled her nose. "He might be dead drunk, but he's still breathing." As she spoke, the halfling let loose with a terrific burp and then lay still again.

"We're going in there?" Driskoll asked, barely controlling a shudder.

Moyra nodded. "If Kruncher's not in there, I'm a two-headed orc."

"Fine," Driskoll sighed. "Have it your way. Get us all killed." He pulled the door open for Moyra and Kellach. "Let's try to make it a quick death at least."

57

Driskoll's boots stuck to the floor as he stepped inside. The entire place reeked of spilled ale, blood, and worse. Lanterns scattered throughout the tavern cast almost as much shadow as light. Smoke from pipes and perhaps something burning in the kitchen wafted through the air. Driskoll hacked, trying to catch his breath.

"Shut that door, boy!" a voice growled from the bar. "You're letting in too much fresh air and light!"

A tankard of ale sailed over Driskoll's head and smashed against the doorframe behind him. He ducked into the main room and let the door swing closed. The crowd booed, then turned back to their drinks.

Driskoll scrambled to catch up with Moyra and Kellach, who were making their way through the main room.

"This is madness," Driskoll hissed. "We're sure to have our throats cut here."

"We will if you keep talking like that," Moyra said through a fake smile. Every eye in the place fell upon Moyra as they passed. Her flaming red hair was impossible to ignore, even through the cloying smoke. She waved to many of the people.

"They know you?" Driskoll said.

"They know my dad," Moyra said.

"Ask them about Kruncher," Kellach said.

Moyra shook her head and whispered, "That would make them suspicious. They might know my dad, but that only goes so far unless there's gold involved."

"But there isn't," Driskoll said.

"Exactly. As soon as I start asking after someone, they'll assume that it involves business. Here, business involves gold— or coins of some sort. It's like blood for a shark."

"And we're standing in the ocean," said Kellach.

The kids wound through the tables to the back of the main room and down a sloping hallway. They passed through at least two different kitchens, past a foul-smelling privy, and into a maze of rooms beyond.

Each chamber the kids entered was different and even stranger than the last. In one large chamber, a pair of centaurs leg-wrestled while spectators tossed wagers back and forth. In the next room, bat-winged people hung upside down from the rafters as they batted around a glowing pufferfish.

In a tiny room, pixies boated about in a gigantic bowl full of steaming mead. Now and then, one hopped from a gondola-shaped leaf to frolic in the fragrant drink.

Fascinated, Driskoll stopped for a moment to peer down at the tiny creatures as they spun about, over, and under the mead. He closed his eyes and breathed in the mead's thick steam through his nose. The scent filled his head with warm thoughts until one of the pixies flew up and belched in his face.

The smell of the creature's roiling stomach sent Driskoll reeling back. The pixies tittered as he went. Driskoll's head was still spinning as Kellach grabbed him by the arm and pulled him along.

"This is no time to be making new friends," Kellach said as they raced to catch up with Moyra.

They walked up and down countless sets of stairs, some straight, others twisting, some short, others long. They even ended up outside once, in a space lost between the surrounding buildings. Someone had set up a pair of chairs and a tiny table off in one corner, and a tiny sign sat there, reading "Private" in a gentle hand.

Driskoll considered stealing a piece of bread from the table so he could leave a trail of crumbs behind them. Sadly, the sight of a pair of rats tussling in the darkness convinced him that such an effort would be futile.

By the time Moyra came to a stop in a smoky chamber, Driskoll was thoroughly turned around. She crooked a finger to beckon the boys closer and pointed.

Before the trio, in a little alcove some would have passed by in the dimness, there was a low table with a handful of chairs around it. The room was empty except for one person: Kruncher.

"There you are!" Moyra shouted. "You're not easy to find. I had to look all over this place."

"You!" Kruncher snarled. "Gotta lotta nerve showin' up here."

"Really?" Moyra smiled. "Aren't you the one who should be paying his debt to society right now? I'd think you'd be more worried about being spotted than I would."

"Paid it off, I did." Kruncher started to stand up. Moyra leaped up on the table, shoving it forward and sloshing Kruncher's foamy, green drink. The edge of the table pinned the half-orc into the alcove. Kruncher was trapped.

"Get off my table!" the half-orc said.

Moyra kneeled down and poked Kruncher in the chest with her finger. "You're not in charge of this little chat, mister."

The half-orc looked as if his head was about to burst. No one had ever talked to him this way before.

"You see those two boys over there?" Moyra said, shoving a thumb toward Kellach and Driskoll. "Do you know who they are?"

Kruncher squinted at them through the haze, then nodded. "Right. Punks from last night. Got me caught, they did."

"More to the point, you ignorant donkey, do you know who their father is?"

"I don't know that he needs to know that," Driskoll said, hoping to cut Moyra off.

Moyra ignored Driskoll. "Ever hear of a man named Torin?" Kruncher shook his head, his eyes dull and blank. "The captain of the watch?" A light flickered in Kruncher's eyes then, and a savage grin spread across his face.

"Owe you, girl," Kruncher grunted. "Bring me boys to beat. Their poppa gonna miss them."

Kellach and Driskoll backed up as Kruncher reached down with both hands to throw over the table. Driskoll looked around for some way to escape, even though he had no idea how to get back to the front door—or any other door at all. Then Moyra poked the half-orc in the eye. Kruncher howled in pain and let go of the table edge as he raised his hands to protect his face.

"Pay attention here!" Moyra said. "This is important. You may not have known who these boys are, but a lot of other people do, including many of those here in the Cat. If you harm a hair on their heads, I'll make sure that everyone here knows you were seen chatting with them last night. Do you know what that means?"

Kruncher rubbed his eye and shook his head.

"It means you're a snitch, at least as far as everyone in town is concerned. And you know what they do to snitches around here?"

On that point, at least, Kruncher was clear. He glared at Moyra out of his good eye and said, "What you want?"

Kellach stepped forward. "Where were you last night?"

Kruncher laughed. "Prison."

"And once you got out?"

"Home."

"Liar!" Driskoll shouted.

Kruncher looked at Driskoll as if he was sizing him up for a meal. Apparently the boy didn't seem like more than a mouthful to him, since Kruncher decided he could ignore him.

"Don't waste our time," Kellach told Kruncher. "We've got you dead to rights."

"How?"

Kellach pointed down at Kruncher's hands. "You still have both your paws. It looks like someone let you out free of charge. How'd you pull that off?"

"Went to Zendric's last night," Kruncher finally said.

Kellach smiled triumphantly. "How did you kill him?"

Kruncher sniggered. "Found globe. Had gold bands. Took it. Used it."

"That explains how someone like you could defeat Zendric," said Moyra.

"How did you know about the device?" Kellach asked.

Kruncher tapped his chest. "Hidden talents. Papa was cleric. Taught me runes."

Driskoll rolled his eyes and looked at Kellach. Kellach was deep in thought.

"The device must kill by releasing the victim's soul," Kellach said, rubbing his chin.

Driskoll shuddered. "No wonder Zendric didn't want you messing with it."

Kellach nodded. "Still, if we can find it, maybe we can reverse the effects."

The young wizard leaned in toward Kruncher again. "This is important, Kruncher. Where is the device now?"

Kruncher snorted. "Dunno."

Moyra poked Kruncher in the eye again. The thug yelped. "If you don't tell us where that thing is," Moyra said, "I'm going to start screaming for help."

Kruncher leaned into Moyra's face. "No one cares."

Unperturbed, Moyra said, "Patch will care. He's my godfather."

Kruncher blanched, then sat back down. "Sold it," he said.

Kellach bowed his head before he spoke. The words came out quiet but clear. "To whom?"

Kruncher snickered. "Fortune hunters downstairs."

"Gods," Driskoll whispered.

"Where are they now?" Kellach asked.

"Gone." Kruncher's smile nearly split his face in half. He began to laugh.

"They left right after you sold them the device?"

Kruncher nodded between his loud, obnoxious guffaws. He couldn't catch enough air to even say "yes."

Moyra climbed down off the table. "Let's go," she said.

Kruncher's malicious laughter echoed down the stairwell as if it were chasing them. "What do we do now?" Driskoll asked.

Moyra spoke up. "Follow me."

CHAPTER

8

Moyra led the way back out of the Skinned Cat. She seemed like she could have managed it blindfolded on a moonless night.

The pixies now floated in their drinks, wide grins plastered on their faces. One of them belched again as the kids passed by, sending the lot of them into fits of giggles.

When the kids got to the front room, Moyra stopped at the bar. She reached over the slab of pitted oak and tugged on the bartender's sleeve.

The bartender was a dark-haired, horse-faced elf. Long ago he had lost an eye and most of an ear in a battle that took place before even Torin's parents were born. A silver patch covered the eye but did little to hide the still-livid scar. It ran from the elf's ruined ear and beneath the patch until it disappeared into his hairline. A line of pure white hair continued the trajectory for a few inches before terminating at the top of the elf's skull.

Most elves were beautiful creatures, almost unearthly in their physical perfection. This creature had been ugly before he was maimed. Now he was actually frightening.

At the sight of the girl, the elf dropped the tankard of ale he'd been pouring. He wrapped his arms around Moyra and hauled her into the air. Moyra squealed with delight.

"My favorite goddaughter!" the elf said. He sat Moyra down atop the bar. "It's been far too long."

"Last I looked, Patch, I was your *only* goddaughter." Moyra beamed at the elf.

"What can I do for you?" Patch asked.

"I need your help. My friends and I were just talking with someone upstairs, a half-orc by the name of Kruncher."

"Ah, yes," Patch nodded. "I serve a lot of hard drinks to a lot of hard people in this place, but that one's just mean. Fated for an early end, if you ask me."

"One can only hope," muttered Kellach.

Moyra ignored him. "This Kruncher had something we were looking for, but he claims to have sold it to a group of adventurers that were in here this morning."

In a low voice, Patch said, "This thing you're looking for, it was a glass globe banded in gold?"

"That's it!" Driskoll said.

Patch favored the boy with half a smile. "Kruncher spent most of the morning shopping that thing around here before he finally got a taker. I doubt he got a tenth of what it was worth. But he's not exactly the most reliable vendor now, is he?"

"Do you know who bought it?" Moyra asked.

"Not well. They were new in town. They kept asking about the ruins, but most people wouldn't talk to them. No sense in helping fools to their deaths now, is there?

"What did they look like?" asked Kellach.

"There were four of them: a couple warriors, a priest, and a traps man, by the look of them. They had a pair of henchmen to carry their gear too. They said they'd heard rumors about the dungeons below the ruins. Visions of fortune and glory in their head, I'm sure. Had those once myself." Patch's hand rubbed the white line that ran through his hair.

"So they're headed for the ruins," Kellach said, mostly to himself.

"That'd be my guess," said Patch. "I'm sorry I couldn't be more help to you children, but it seems that thing of yours is gone."

"Because no one would go after it in the ruins?" Driskoll said.

Patch looked at Driskoll as if the boy might be simple. "You'd have to be desperate—or crazy."

Moyra leaned over and kissed Patch on his scarred cheek. "Thank you, Patch! You've been a great help." With that, she slid down from the bar and led the boys to the door.

Patch rubbed the spot Moyra had kissed and said, "Anytime, lass, anytime. Don't be a stranger now. I want to see you back here before your father's release party."

"Promise," Moyra called as she slipped out the door. Kellach and Driskoll ran after her.

"What now?" Driskoll said. "We can't really be thinking of going to the ruins."

"Why not?" said Moyra. "It's the middle of the day. If we hurry, we might be able to catch them before they enter the dungeons. Some fortune hunters make camp in the ruins above."

"Good point," said Kellach as he started walking again, beckoning for the others to keep up. "Maybe we can catch up with them there."

"But the city gate is in the other direction!" Driskoll said as he trotted along behind.

"We're stopping at home first," Kellach said. "For a trip to the shattered city, we should be prepared."

Kellach didn't fool his little brother for a moment. Driskoll knew what he was planning. If they didn't find the fortune hunters in the ruins, Kellach would press on into the dungeons without hesitation.

Driskoll sighed. Either way, they would need to gather some supplies.

When the trio reached Kellach and Driskoll's home, the place was empty.

Kellach walked straight into Torin's bedroom. He shoved aside the dressing screen in front of the closet and tugged on the door.

"It's locked!" said Kellach. A large, thick padlock hung from a new hasp across the door's edge, sealing it tight. The lock looked like one of the kind used to seal the cells in the Curston prison. "When did he get around to putting that on the door?"

"Probably after the time you borrowed his sword to practice 'enchanting' it," Driskoll said.

"You don't 'enchant' swords," Kellach said, irritated. "You 'imbue them with magic.' And anyhow, it was an old sword. He wouldn't have missed it."

"If it hadn't embedded itself in his headboard. While he was sleeping."

"That's beside the point."

As the brothers bickered, Moyra studied the lock. "It's simple," she said. She reached into a deep pocket in her jacket, rummaged around a bit, and pulled out a thin iron bar with a curve on one end.

"That's a bit large for picking locks," Kellach said.

"And a bit small if you're planning to bash the door down," Driskoll said.

Moyra smirked. She stepped forward and stuck the bar's curved end under one of the metal strips holding the lock in place. With two deft moves, she pried up the nails holding down the strip. The door swung wide.

Kellach and Driskoll stood there stunned.

"It's customary to say 'thanks,' " Moyra said. She gestured for them to enter the closet like a shopkeeper inviting children into a candy store.

The brothers said, "Thanks," then leaped into the closet.

After a good deal of poking about, the kids managed to come up with everything they thought they might need: lanterns, flint and tinder, a knife for each of them, and backpacks to carry all sorts of other odds and ends, including some rope.

"You never know when you're going to need some rope," said Moyra. "At least that's what my dad always says."

On the way out, the kids stopped to raid the pantry. They each stuffed their packs with bread, cheese, and a skin full of water.

As Driskoll was buckling up his pack, he noticed Kellach slipping a thin book into his bag. "You're bringing your spell-book?" he asked. "I thought Zendric forbade you to carry that anywhere but between home and school."

"Zendric's dead," Kellach said. "At least for now."

Driskoll shrugged. He knew Kellach had already memorized a number of spells this morning. The only reason Kellach would want his spellbook was if he thought he'd need to consult it tomorrow. It had been their mother's first spellbook, and Kellach often carried it with him, although not as secretly as he hoped.

■ ▮ ▮ ▮ ▮

It was a long hike to the ruins, along a wide but neglected road. The path branched off the main highway about a mile past the tall, thick walls surrounding Curston. Word around Curston had it that the road was lousy with adventurers roaming back and forth between the ruins and the town.

But Kellach, Moyra, and Driskoll met no one else on the road. It was strangely quiet. They saw no signs of any animals other than a few birds circling lazily overhead.

"Are those hawks?" Driskoll wondered aloud.

Kellach looked up at the birds, shading his eyes. "Vultures," he said. "Let's hope we're not too late."

Kellach, Driskoll, and Moyra trudged on. Driskoll's pack seemed heavier with every step. When they set out, they had decided to carry as many supplies as they could. Now, though, Driskoll couldn't remember why this had seemed like a good idea. He considered tossing the heavy lantern in his pack to the side of the road. Why waste strength carrying something he'd likely not need?

A couple of miles down the road, the trio came to the ruins. Vines and other plants covered the ancient city's walls. Long before the city came to be, a forest had stood here. It almost seemed that the forest had reclaimed the place once again. The road ended at the place where the city's legendary bronze gates had once stood.

"Careful now," Kellach warned. "You never know who—or what—might be watching."

This was a thought that hadn't struck Driskoll before then. Suddenly his head filled with visions of evil creatures of all sorts. He looked behind him and half expected to find an arrow sticking out of his pack.

Kellach stopped to look around, but Moyra marched right on through the gateway.

"My dad used to come here sometimes to try his luck. He said that the best place to enter the dungeon is down a stairwell in the center of the main square."

"Where is that?" Kellach asked.

Moyra stood up on her toes for a moment and looked around in every direction. Finally, she pointed off to the west and said, "There! You see the top of that crumbling tower over there? That was once the city's astronomical clock. The square is right in front of it."

"Excellent," Kellach said as he started walking in that direction.

As the kids got closer to the square, they could hear sounds coming from it. At first, the sounds were hard to identify: clanging pans, rattling blades, a suit of armor coming apart. Then they heard the voices.

The trio padded toward the voices, up a small slope on the outer edge of the square. The hill crested against the remnants of a large building. Buildings had once surrounded the square. Now most of them were nothing but crumbling stone.

Driskoll looked over the edge of the wall. From this side, it was a ten-foot drop to the ground. But Driskoll could see the adjoining wall was low enough for them to scramble over. Across from him, the building's far wall contained a small window, looking out onto the square.

Without speaking, Driskoll pointed to the path that ran down the hill to the right. The kids followed it around the building's corner and jumped over the shorter wall, into the building's remains. Then they crept toward the small window overgrown with vines and peeked through the leaves into the square.

The square stood roughly fifty yards across in each direction. Driskoll spotted a set of crumbled statues at the center, toppled into a stone ring that had once been a bubbling fountain, the city's centerpiece. Now it was barely more than rubble.

A handful of creatures roamed about the square, bickering with each other. Short and spindly, they were little larger than gnomes, but their orange skin and sharp fangs marked them as a race apart. They wore dirty rags under poorly arranged leather strips and swung small, spiked clubs as a constant threat.

"Ugly little things, aren't they?" Moyra whispered.

"What are they?" asked Driskoll.

One of the larger creatures grew frustrated with an argument he was having with a smaller fellow. He smashed the smaller creature to the ground with his club. The victim did not get up again.

"Goblins," said Kellach. "Zendric taught me their language. It's not all that far from Draconic."

A few goblins poked about the remains of a camp several yards from the fountain. In the dirt next to a still-burning cooking fire lay a couple of men, short black arrows jutting from their backs.

"Do you think those are the fortune hunters we're looking for?" asked Moyra.

"If they are, they're the worst I've ever heard of," said Driskoll. "Being felled by a few goblins before you even enter the dungeon is not the stuff of legends."

"What are we going to do?" asked Moyra. "Those orange-skinned, big-eared runts are standing between us and the camp. Should we try to run them off before they find the globe?"

Kellach held up his hand to slow Moyra down. "Let's come up with some sort of plan first." Before he could say another word, though, two arrows whizzed past and stuck in a rotted, half-folded support beam in front of the kids. They turned around to see a pair of goblins looking down from the tall wall behind them.

As the goblins each nocked another arrow to their bows, they screamed one word again and again.

"What are they saying?" Driskoll asked.

Kellach was kind enough to translate. "They're saying 'Attack!'"

CHAPTER

9

"Do something!" Driskoll said to Kellach. "Cast something!"
"Hold on!" Kellach yelled as he rummaged around in his pack. "I've got some spells memorized, but I need the right ingredients to make them work." Moyra and Driskoll scrambled over the low wall at the side of the building, out of sight of the goblin archers. An arrow sailed over Driskoll's head, and another slammed right into Kellach's pack.

Kellach yelped, and there was a low, popping sound. When Driskoll stood up to see what had happened, Kellach was sputtering and wet. The arrow had pierced his waterskin.

"You little orange bundles of rot!" Kellach thundered. The goblin archers were so stunned by this outburst that they stopped to stare at him for a moment.

With the goblins distracted, Moyra grabbed Driskoll by the arm and led him back along the outside of the wall, crouching as they scrambled around the side of the hill. Quietly as they could, they circled around the archers and came up the low hill behind them.

Kellach was still yelling at the goblins. "My spellbook is wet!" he shouted. "My mother's spellbook!"

The goblins made a strange sort of rasping sound in the back of their throats. When Moyra and Driskoll finally got up behind them, the kids saw the goblins holding their bellies, and they realized the creatures were laughing at Kellach's antics.

"You think that's funny?" Kellach shouted. "Try laughing off this!"

He ran toward the goblins, shaking his clenched fist. They fell silent for a moment as they looked down at him, far out of reach. Then they glanced at each other and burst out laughing again.

As Kellach neared the foot of the wall, he started chanting, and their laughter stopped. The archers each nocked another arrow for Kellach, but before they could draw their bows, he stopped speaking and made a strange gesture with his hands. It was almost like he was tapping one of the goblins between the eyes, although from yards away.

The archer suddenly let his arms fall to his sides. His compatriot stopped to watch a thin line of drool spill out of the stunned goblin's wide, toothy mouth.

"Now!" Moyra shouted. Before Driskoll knew what she was doing, she leaped forward and shoved the drool-free goblin off the wall. He flailed his arms as he fell and landed with a sickening crunch.

By the time Driskoll reached the other goblin, the creature was starting to recover from Kellach's spell. The goblin reached over to stab at Moyra with the arrow in his hand, but before the blow landed, Driskoll barreled into his waist and knocked him flying down after his friend.

Kellach yelled in surprise as the second goblin nearly came down on top of him. Moyra and Driskoll whooped in triumph, but their victory was short-lived.

As the two friends cheered, four other goblins clambered atop the ruined wall facing the square. They were not as amused as their friends had been.

Kellach drew his knife and dashed over to where the two fallen goblins lay. The one that Moyra had shoved off the wall was unconscious but still breathing. The other's right arm was twisted at a wrong angle. He was holding it and screeching in his strange language. Kellach jumped behind the screaming goblin and held his knife before the creature's face. The goblin instantly shut its mouth tight.

"Stand back!" Kellach shouted in the common tongue before repeating himself in Goblin. He shoved the tip of his borrowed knife toward his hostage's throat to punctuate his order.

One of the goblins raised his bow and shot an arrow into the unconscious goblin, puncturing its chest. The poor creature let out a yelp and then lay still.

"I don't think they care much about their friend!" Driskoll yelled down.

"Good point!" Kellach said. He tried to crouch further behind his hostage. He'd dropped the knife at this point, no longer bothering to bluff that he would have ever harmed a helpless creature. He used both arms to hold the injured goblin before him, hoping it would do him some good.

Moyra managed to find a fist-sized rock, and she launched it at the goblin who had shot the arrow. It smacked him in the head, knocking him off balance.

Before the tippy goblin could right himself, Driskoll hurled a rock of his own at the creature. This one glanced off the goblin's hip. He slipped off the wall and out of sight.

While the other goblins watched their friend fall, Moyra and Driskoll peppered them with a hail of stones. From his landing spot in the main square, the fallen goblin screeched something at his fellows. The three remaining creatures on the wall hopped off after him.

"Wonderful!" Kellach yelled. "They're running away!"

Moyra and Driskoll whooped it up some more as they raced back around to where Kellach still held his hostage in his hands. When they reached Kellach, they saw the dead goblin lying there too and fell silent.

"They really killed him?" Driskoll asked, looking down at the creature's now-pale body.

"I'm afraid so," Kellach nodded grimly. "This isn't a game. The ruins are as deadly as the legends say."

Driskoll knew that the goblins would have killed any of them, given the chance. He still felt sorry for the creature, betrayed by his so-called friends.

At the sight of Moyra and Driskoll, the goblin in Kellach's grasp renewed his efforts to twist his way to freedom. Every move, though, caused him to gasp in pain from his broken arm. Between those gasps, he screeched desperately, calling after the compatriots who had abandoned him. Whether he was pleading for help or cursing them, Driskoll could not tell—perhaps both.

Moyra pointed her knife at the goblin's neck, and he fell silent once again. "What shall we do with you?" she asked, more to herself than him.

"We can't just kill him," Driskoll said, surprising himself with the strength of his voice.

"Why not?" Moyra said. "It's Broken Town justice. If someone tries to kill you, it's self-defense, no matter when it happens."

"He's not attacking us now," said Kellach.

Moyra nodded. "You're still holding him down."

Kellach released the goblin, leaping away as he did, wary of any tricks. The goblin looked up at him with fear in his eyes. Holding his hurt arm, the creature fell to its spindly knees and began sobbing.

Moyra readied her knife for a killing blow. "It's a trick," she said.

Kellach stepped between Moyra and the goblin. "We're not killing him," he said. "He's no danger to us."

"He shot at you! He tried to kill you! They all did."

"But they failed. Anyway, we're not goblins, are we?"

Moyra stomped her foot. "You're insane! We let him go, and he'll be back here again with a score of his friends."

"They might come back anyhow," Kellach pointed out, "whether we kill him or not."

Moyra glowered at Kellach. Driskoll thought she might try to use her knife on the young apprentice first and then finish off the goblin. Neither one of them was prepared to budge an inch. The goblin kneeled there staring up at them, perhaps astonished he wasn't already dead.

"Let's put it to a vote," Driskoll said. "That's fair, right?"

Both Moyra and Kellach looked at him like the younger boy had turned into a goblin before their eyes.

"You're crazy!" said Moyra.

"This isn't negotiable," said Kellach.

"Look," Driskoll said, "we're all in this together, right? It's the only way we have a chance to find Zendric's globe."

The others nodded. The goblin, seeming to begin to understand, nodded too.

"If we're together on this, then we should vote. We work as a group, and we make decisions as a group."

"We're no Knights of the Silver Dragon," Kellach said.

"What in the gods' darkest names are you babbling about?" said Moyra. As she spoke, she noticed the goblin edging farther away from them. She pointed her knife at him again, and he stopped cold.

"Just like any group, the Knights used to disagree about things," Kellach explained. "When they did, they put the matter to a vote and were all bound by it, just like what Driskoll proposed. It's what held them together for hundreds of years."

"Right now, I'll settle for sticking together until we get back home," Driskoll said. Both Moyra and Kellach nodded at that.

"All right," said Moyra. "I'm in."

Driskoll and Moyra both looked at Kellach, who squinted at each of them. "Me too."

"Then let's vote on the goblin's fate," Driskoll said. "All in favor of letting the goblin go, raise your hand."

Kellach and Driskoll each raised a hand high. Moyra stared at them both in disbelief, then said, "Fine. Have it your way."

Kellach reached out and grabbed the goblin by his good arm, hauling him to his feet. He said something to the injured creature in the Goblin tongue. The creature's jaw dropped, and he stood there for a moment, not able to understand what Kellach was telling him.

Kellach repeated himself, and the goblin shook his head in disbelief. Moyra reached over and jabbed the creature in the rump with the hilt of her knife, and he jumped nearly a foot. He turned to look at each of the kids.

When Driskoll waved good-bye at the goblin, a wide smile spread across the creature's face. The goblin nodded a quick thanks, said something in his coarse tongue, and then fled.

As the kids watched, the goblin leaped through the vine-covered window, tearing the plants down with him as he hit the ground on the other side. He yelped, then jumped back up, holding his injured arm. He glanced back at the kids and then sprinted away at top speed.

"What did he say?" asked Driskoll.

"I'm not sure. 'Till we meet again,' I think," said Kellach.

Moyra spat on the ground. "Let's hope that never happens."

The goblin ran straight through the remains of the camp and disappeared down a stairwell in the center of the square. The three friends watched him go, then made their way to the camp to look around.

Kellach examined the two bodies near the campfire. The first was that of a young man, not much older than Kellach, with short hair the color of dirt. His chin bore the start of a weak beard. The other man's hair had thinned to almost nothing atop his head. His beard was trimmed and gray as a rain cloud. Several short, black arrows stuck out of their backs.

"They're dead," Kellach announced.

"Where are the rest of them?" Moyra asked.

Kellach pointed toward the stairwell where the goblin had disappeared.

"We missed them," said Driskoll. "They must have gone straight in."

Moyra started rummaging through the remains of the camp. When she reached the dead men, she patted down their clothes and turned out their pockets. She noticed the boys watching her. "Give me a hand."

"What are you doing?" Driskoll asked, hoping she didn't expect him to touch a dead body.

"What are we here for?" Moyra said, rolling her eyes. "I'm looking for the globe."

Kellach and Driskoll pitched in straight away. They searched through every inch of the place. Nothing was left unturned, but they came up empty.

"It's not here," Driskoll said, discouraged. "The other fortune hunters must have it."

"These men didn't even have swords," Moyra said, pointing down at the two bodies. "They must be the henchmen Patch mentioned. The other four must still be in the dungeon."

Kellach turned toward the others. "We have to go in after it."

"You're nuts," Driskoll said. "We're just a bunch of kids."

"It's the only hope we have of getting Zendric's soul back in time. A body can only go without its soul for so long before the connection is severed forever. The clock is ticking."

"I don't think Zendric would want us to die," Driskoll said.

"We're not going to die."

Driskoll pointed over at the dead men. "I'll bet they thought the same thing this morning."

"All right, then," Kellach said, "have it your way. We'll put it to a vote."

"Fine!" Driskoll said. "All in favor of rushing into certain death to save the life of an old elf who might actually be dead already?"

Kellach raised his hand. Driskoll kept both hands down. The brothers looked to Moyra to break the tie.

"Did I ever tell you about my last birthday?" Moyra asked.

"What does this have to do with the vote?" Driskoll said.

"My dad had been in prison for just over a month, and my mother was having trouble making ends meet. She wasn't even going to be able to bake a cake for me, she thought.

"That night, a knock came on the door, and I ran to open it. My father was standing there, a cake in one hand and a bag of coins in the other. We were so happy to see him, we didn't even ask how or why.

"At the end of the night, though, Dad told us that he had to go back to his cell. He had been granted one night of freedom, but only under the condition that he return the same night to finish out his sentence. Do you know who set him free?"

The boys both shook their heads.

"It was Zendric." Moyra raised her hand. "We're going in."

"This is beyond madness," Driskoll said as he followed Kellach and Moyra toward the stairwell. "I've heard lots of stories about people going into this place, and not one of them ever turned out well."

"Zendric would go in after any of us," Kellach said. "We can hardly do less."

Driskoll saw the determination in Kellach and Moyra's eyes and let loose a deep sigh. "Let's get it over with."

"It'll be darker than a new moon down there," said Moyra. She dug into her pack and pulled out a couple of torches. She lit them both and handed one to Driskoll. Kellach lit the lantern they'd borrowed from Torin's closet.

The three friends nodded at each other, then walked down the long stairs into the dungeons. At the bottom of the stairwell, an open doorway beckoned, promising adventure beyond. Someone had scrawled out a sign and posted it over the door long ago.

"TURN BACK!" it read.

They walked past the sign without a word.

CHAPTER

10

Inside the underground complex, the corridors were wide and well built. The arched ceilings were beyond even Kellach's reach, but just barely. Both the ceiling and the walls were made of fitted stone reinforced here and there with buttresses.

"It's supposed to be like a maze in here," Kellach said. "Maybe we should map it as we go."

"My father told me that the best thing to do in a place like this is to always bear left," Moyra said. "If you do that, you can always find your way back."

Driskoll had expected the place to be filled with dust and cobwebs, but there must have been enough traffic through the area to keep anything from building up. What he did see were stains and spatters on the walls. They looked like blood.

The kids wandered around the halls for what seemed like an endless time, always keeping to the left. They found evidence of people recently passing through: burnt-out torches, empty ration kits, and so on.

"Do you think this stuff belonged to the people we're looking for?" Driskoll asked.

Kellach reached down to touch one of the torches. "I'd say so. This torch is still warm." The trio turned a corner and continued on down a long hallway.

After only a few steps, Moyra stopped short.

"Hold it!" she yelled. She reached forward, grabbed the back of Kellach's shirt, and pulled. He found himself with one foot hanging out over a wide pit. He slowly brought his foot back and stepped away from the edge of the dark hole.

Kellach held the lantern high so they could get a better look at the pit. It ran across the entire width of the hallway. It must have been at least ten feet to the other side, where the corridor continued on. A moth-eaten sheet of gray fabric that had once covered the pit hung in tatters from its edges.

"That's a long leap," Driskoll said.

"It's more than a leap," Kellach said. "With all this gear, it's almost impossible."

"Do you notice how the ceiling suddenly drops here?" Moyra asked.

"Is that what tipped you off?" Kellach asked.

Moyra nodded. "Places like this are filled with traps of all sorts. My dad is the best in Curston at spotting them. He told me about things like these. They lower the ceiling so if you try to jump over the pit you smack your head and fall in."

"So there's no way across," Kellach said.

"Not unless you want to try to rig up something with your ropes. The walls aren't very smooth."

"How deep is this thing?" Driskoll asked. Peering into the darkness at the bottom of the pit, it seemed like it might go on forever.

"There's one way to find out," Moyra said. She picked up a loose stone from the floor and tossed it into the pit. In an instant, they heard it hit bottom.

Moyra fished the torch out of her pack and tied a coil of thin rope around the torch's handle. Moyra held the torch out over the rim of the pit and slowly lowered it down.

They peered over the edge to see what the light revealed. The bottom of the pit was covered with tall, nasty spikes—more like metal-tipped spears—and two bodies hung impaled on them. One of the bodies looked like it might have been there for years. Its empty eye sockets stared up at the kids blankly. The other was fresh. A dark circle of blood still pooled below it.

Moyra said a quick prayer under her breath as she peered down at the fresh corpse. "From the way his body's angled, he was coming from the other direction. He must have been in a hurry not to see this open pit."

"If he fell in from the other side, there must be another way around," Kellach said.

"We can cross here," Moyra said.

"Don't you see the pit in front of us?" said Driskoll. "A climber like you might be able to scoot along the wall above those spikes, but I'm not going to try it."

Moyra shook her head. "There's an easier way. We just climb down into the pit on this side and then up the other."

"What about the spikes?"

"There aren't any along the edges," Kellach said. "Whoever built this probably wanted to be able to get across it in a pinch. In fact, you can see handholds carved into the stones on either side."

"There are two bodies down there," said Driskoll.

"They're dead," said Moyra. "They can't hurt you."

With that, Moyra handed Driskoll the rope and lowered herself into the pit. It was only about ten feet deep, but when she was on the bottom she seemed as distant as those vultures circling the ruins.

Moyra grabbed the torch at the end of the rope and untied it. Driskoll hauled the rope up and recoiled it, then stuffed it in his pack. As he did, Moyra leaned over through the spikes to get a better look at the two victims impaled there.

When Moyra brought the torch close to the most recent victim, she could see that the spikes running through him were still wet with his blood. The look of pained horror on the man's face made her shiver. She steeled herself and reached out to make a blessing for the poor man's soul.

Moyra tiptoed past the first corpse and came to where the other body hung suspended on the spikes. This hapless soul wore both armor and a helmet, although neither had done much to protect him from the force of his full weight falling on the spikes. He still bore a longsword at the end of his outstretched arm.

Moyra brought the torch up over the body to get a better look at it. The flesh had mostly rotted off the man's frame long ago, leaving a dusty husk where a living, breathing person once had been. Its eye sockets stood open and empty, and its receded lips exposed its teeth, revealing a deathly grin.

Moyra reached out to make a blessing once again, although the soul of this man was no doubt long gone. As she did, the corpse dropped its blade and reached out to grab her by the wrist.

Moyra screamed, weakly at first and then at the top of her lungs. She pulled and yanked to get free, but the creature's grip was as unforgiving as a vise. As she fought with it, the undead thing struggled to free itself from the spikes on which it rested. Instead of rising up, though, it worked its body farther down onto them.

Desperate, Moyra smacked the creature with the torch, bashing the horrid thing about the head and shoulders with the blazing stick. It opened its mouth and silently laughed.

Moyra saw her chance. She shoved the burning end of her torch straight into the creature's mouth. The thing's head burst into flames, and its quiet laughter turned to screams. It let loose Moyra's hand, and she pulled free and scrambled back toward the boys and up the side of the pit.

Both Kellach and Driskoll reached down to help Moyra up. As soon as they got hold of her, they hauled her up the rest of the way.

Driskoll looked down into the pit to see that the creature had managed to haul itself free from the spikes. Its head still ablaze, it reached for the side of the pit and pulled itself up after the three friends.

Tell us what you think about *Secret of the Spiritkeeper!* Please answer the following questions and mail the card to us.

1. Overall, how would you rate *Secret of the Spiritkeeper?*

	Excellent				Poor
Overall	☐ 5	☐ 4	☐ 3	☐ 2	☐ 1

2. How would you rate *Secret of the Spiritkeeper* on each of the following features?

FEATURE	Excellent				Poor
Cover art	☐ 5	☐ 4	☐ 3	☐ 2	☐ 1
Back cover	☐ 5	☐ 4	☐ 3	☐ 2	☐ 1
Title	☐ 5	☐ 4	☐ 3	☐ 2	☐ 1
Story	☐ 5	☐ 4	☐ 3	☐ 2	☐ 1
Price	☐ 5	☐ 4	☐ 3	☐ 2	☐ 1

3. Where did you first see this book?
☐ Bookstore shelf
☐ School library
☐ Public library
☐ Internet store
☐ Other, please specify:_____

4. How did you get this book? Did you...? (choose one)
☐ Buy it yourself with your own money
☐ Have a parent, grandparent or someone else buy it for you when you were in the store together
☐ Receive it as a gift
☐ Other, please specify:_____

5. Please rank each of the following five items according to how important it is to you in choosing a book to buy – 1 means it is the most important factor in choosing a book, 2 means it is the next most, etc., and 5 means it is the least important factor. (Please use each number between 1 and 5 only once.)

Factor	Rank
Author	_____
Cover	_____
Series	_____
Recommendations from librarians/booksellers	_____
Recommendations from friends/relatives	_____

6. Which of the following elements do you look for in a novel? (mark all that apply)
☐ Action
☐ Humor
☐ Interesting stories
☐ Magic
☐ Mystery
☐ Romance
☐ Well-developed characters
☐ Other, please specify:_____

7. How would you rate your interest in the following types of novels?

	Very Interested				Not at all Interested
Action/Adventure (like books by Gary Paulsen or Will Hobbs)	☐ 5	☐ 4	☐ 3	☐ 2	☐ 1
Fantasy (like *Lord of the Rings, Harry Potter,* etc.)	☐ 5	☐ 4	☐ 3	☐ 2	☐ 1
Horror (like the *Goosebumps* series or books by Neil Gaiman)	☐ 5	☐ 4	☐ 3	☐ 2	☐ 1
Humorous adventure (like the Lemony Snicket books or *Captain Underpants*)	☐ 5	☐ 4	☐ 3	☐ 2	☐ 1
Mystery (like *Nancy Drew* or *Sammy Keyes*)	☐ 5	☐ 4	☐ 3	☐ 2	☐ 1
Romance (like the *Sweet Valley High* or *Princess Diaries* series)	☐ 5	☐ 4	☐ 3	☐ 2	☐ 1
Space adventure (like *Star Wars*)	☐ 5	☐ 4	☐ 3	☐ 2	☐ 1

8. Which of the following types of novels is your favorite? (choose only one)
☐ Adventure (like books by Gary Paulsen or Will Hobbs)
☐ Fantasy (like *Lord of the Rings, Harry Potter,* etc.)
☐ Horror (like the *Goosebumps* series or books by Neil Gaiman)
☐ Humorous adventure (like the Lemony Snicket books or *Captain Underpants*)
☐ Mystery (like *Nancy Drew* or *Sammy Keyes*)
☐ Romance (like the *Sweet Valley High* or *Princess Diaries* series)
☐ Space adventure (like *Star Wars*)
☐ Other, please specify:_____

9. Who is your favorite author? (please write in the author's name)
_____

10. What types of fiction do you read regularly? (Check all that apply)
☐ Action/Adventure (like books by Gary Paulsen or Will Hobbs)
☐ Horror (like the *Goosebumps* series or books by Neil Gaiman)
☐ Classic literature (like *Ramona Quimby* or *Tuck Everlasting*)
☐ Mystery (like *Nancy Drew* or *Sammy Keyes* series)
☐ Fantasy (like *Harry Potter* or *Lord of the Rings*)
☐ Science fiction (like *Star Wars* or *A Wrinkle in Time*)
☐ Historical (like the *Dear America* series or *Bud, Not Buddy*)
☐ Romance (like the *Sweet Valley High* or *Princess Diaries* series)
☐ Other, please specify:_____

11. What is your gender?
☐ Male ☐ Female

12. What is your birth date?
_____ / _____ / _____
Month   Day   Year

Full Name:_____
Address:_____
City:_____ State/Province:_____
Country:_____ ZIP/Postal Code:_____
Phone:_____ Email:_____
☐ Please check here if you DO wish to be contacted or receive promotional offers.

If you are under 13, we must receive permission from a parent in order to contact you or send you promotional offers.

I give permission for my child to be contacted or receive promotional offers from Wizards of the Coast:

Parent's signature

BUSINESS REPLY MAIL

FIRST-CLASS MAIL   PERMIT NO. 609   RENTON, WA

POSTAGE WILL BE PAID BY ADDRESSEE

ATTN.: CONSUMER RESPONSE
WIZARDS OF THE COAST
PO BOX 980
RENTON WA 98057-0980

CHAPTER

11

Driskoll hollered, "Run!"

Kellach led the way, pulling Moyra along behind him. With her other hand, she grabbed Driskoll. The three of them made a chain that raced along the halls, back the way they had come.

As the kids ran, Driskoll looked back. The zombie was hot on their heels, its flaming head standing out sharply from the surrounding darkness.

"It's following us!" he said. They all tried to run faster.

Kellach did his best to pick their way back to the entrance, always going to the right whenever possible. They had walked into the place, though, and now they were running out.

Eventually, the kids missed a turn.

"Kellach, we were supposed to turn back there!" Driskoll yelled.

Kellach looked back over his shoulder and said, "No time!"

The zombie wasn't any faster than the kids. In fact, in a short race against it, each of them could have broken the ribbon first. But it never tired, and it never wavered from its goal.

Driskoll began to get winded. He could feel a stitch starting in his side. Kellach was panting like mad, and Moyra said breathlessly, "We can't keep this up much longer."

Driskoll glanced back, and the zombie's head was no longer ablaze. He couldn't say when the flames had gone out or how. Most of the skin on the thing's skull had fallen away, but what was left glowed as red as the embers of a fire. Coming out of the darkness, it seemed like the head was flying along the corridor after the trio. The only evidence that ruined that illusion was the steady clanking of the thing's armored feet on the stone floor.

"Help!" Driskoll screamed. "Help!"

"What good will that do?" Moyra asked. "You'll bring every other monster in the place down on our heads!"

"It can't make us any more dead!"

Kellach looked back at Moyra, and the two of them joined in Driskoll's chorus. "Help!"

As the kids screamed out their last bits of breath, the hallway opened up into a large chamber that had once been a dining hall. Fragments of tables and chairs were scattered about the place, and the crumbling remnants of a large fireplace still stood in the center of the room. The ceiling climbed so high the light from Kellach's lantern couldn't reach the top.

"What's that?" Moyra said. Driskoll saw a hint of light straight ahead of them.

"It's a lantern," Kellach said, spitting each word out between his labored breaths.

"Why are we heading for it?" Driskoll asked.

"Do you have a better idea?"

Driskoll kept his mouth shut and put every bit of energy he had into his flagging legs. It felt like someone had clapped irons on his ankles, but the *clank-clank-clank* of the zombie's gait kept him pumping along.

As the kids neared the light, Driskoll saw that Kellach was right. The light came from a lantern standing next to the chamber's far wall. The body of a warrior lay next to it.

"It's another one!" Driskoll shouted.

"Help!" Kellach yelled, more desperate than ever. The distance between the warrior and the runners narrowed.

The warrior lifted his head, as if Kellach's shout had woken him from a dream. He reached over to grab the longsword lying beside him and rolled to a seated position. His armor rasped as he pushed against the wall behind him to stand.

"St. Cuthbert!" the man cried. "If this is your will, I commend my soul to your keeping!"

With that, the man shoved off from the wall. He held his sword before him with both hands, its tip raised and ready. He looked as if it cost him every bit of strength to manage it.

"Zombie!" Kellach yelled to the man. "Right behind us!"

In the flickering light, Driskoll saw a savage grin play across the warrior's lips.

As the last yards between the runners and the wall disappeared, the warrior lurched forward, letting loose with an earsplitting battle yell. Kellach ducked to the right, Moyra went left. Driskoll dived forward on his belly and slid between the warrior's legs.

Driskoll turned as he hit the wall, right next to the lantern, and looked up to see the warrior unleash a single savage blow at the zombie's still-glowing head. It struck the creature at the neck, and the red-hot skull sailed off into the darkness where it fell neatly into the fireplace's base.

The rest of the zombie's body collapsed to the ground and fell still, as dead as it should have been. The warrior stood next to the fallen creature. He tottered for a moment, but using his sword as a cane he managed to catch himself. He turned around.

The warrior had no words for the trio, only a wide smile. Then his eyes rolled back into his head, and he toppled to the floor.

CHAPTER

12

All three of the kids raced to the warrior's side. "Is he dead?" Driskoll asked.

Kellach felt the man's throat and knelt down to listen for his breath. "Not yet," he said, "but he's not far off."

At Kellach's direction, he and Driskoll rolled the warrior over onto his back. Moyra scrambled off to fetch the man's lantern.

Having had much experience at helping Torin in and out of his armor, Kellach and Driskoll set to work loosing the warrior from his chainmail. If the scars on his body were to tell the tale, he was a veteran of many campaigns. The kids were determined that he would not die after saving them.

"Fetch his pack," Kellach said to Moyra. Without a word, she obeyed.

While Kellach rummaged about in the man's belongings, Driskoll tended to the wounds. They were mostly superficial—a scratch here, a cut there—but there were a lot of them. Driskoll needed some clean cloth to bind them up. When he glanced behind, he saw Kellach toss a spare shirt out of the warrior's pack. Driskoll grabbed it and started tearing it into strips.

Before Driskoll could even ask for it, Kellach tapped him on the shoulder with the man's waterskin. Driskoll nodded his thanks and took the skin. He used the water to drench two of the strips, and then Moyra and he went to work cleaning the wounds. As they worked on some of the cuts, the man squirmed in pain, but he never cried out once.

"Aha!" Kellach said. Driskoll looked up to see him pluck a handful of vials from the man's pack. They were each made of steel and sealed with a wax-covered cork.

Kellach held the vials up to the lantern light and read the symbols scratched on their surfaces. On the third vial, he stopped and said, "Yes!" He looked through the rest quickly and let all but the third fall to the ground. Then he pulled out his knife, broke the seal on the vial, and uncorked it.

"Open his mouth," Kellach said. Driskoll put his hand under the man's neck and angled his chin up while Moyra pulled open his jaw. Kellach reached over and poured every last drop of the fluid from the vial into the man's mouth.

The stuff smelled horrible, and some it came out of the vial in clumps that nearly choked the warrior as he swallowed them down. "What is this gunk?" Driskoll asked.

Kellach smiled at his brother, then looked down at the warrior. "It's a healing potion, one made by a priest."

As the three kids watched, the wounds on the warrior's skin began to knit together on their own, healing before their eyes. Moyra gasped at the sight, and the warrior groaned. His eyes fluttered and then opened.

At first, the warrior seemed mystified to see the three friends. "Children," he said. "I must still be dreaming." Then he sat up and looked around to see where he was. As his eyes tried to pierce the darkness, the situation dawned on him.

The warrior reached out and plucked the empty vial from Kellach's hand. He looked at it, then Kellach, and smiled. "Clever lad," he said. "I didn't realize that Wencel had slipped that into my pack along with the rest. You've just saved my life."

"We're just returning the favor," Kellach said.

The warrior nodded. "Yes, I seem to recall something about a hot-headed zombie. I thought I dreamed that too."

Moyra pointed over to the fireplace, which now had a light flickering from the bottom of it, and a bit of smoke curling up toward the ceiling. "Your dream has started a fire for us." She laughed. "That was an amazing shot."

"Lucky," the warrior said as he struggled to his feet.

The warrior limped over to the fireplace and sat down on its wide, stone rim. The kids gathered around and did the same. The zombie's head lay there in the center, where it had ignited the fragments of chairs and tables someone had tossed there, perhaps in a futile effort to clean up the room long ago. The warmth of the fire felt good in the cool dungeon air, although the kids were still warm from their long run.

"My name is Durmok," the warrior said. "I don't suppose you've heard of me?" The kids looked at him, and he shook his head. "I am far from home."

Kellach introduced them each by name. Durmok raised his hand to each of them in greeting. "I am pleased to meet you, but you must tell me, what are children doing here in the Dungeons of Doom?"

Driskoll gulped. "Is that what people call this place? To us, these are just the dungeons under the ruins."

"Aye," said Durmok. "The people of Curston don't like to talk of such matters or use such colorful language, but that's what this place is known as far and wide. The name alone is vibrant enough to draw adventurers here from leagues beyond, although none have yet managed to tame the place.

"We—my companions and I—hoped to be the first to manage it. It seems that is not to be."

"We found two men dead at your camp," Driskoll said. "The goblins shot them."

Durmok cursed. "Those goblins and their chief!" he said. "That is where our fortune turned. The moment Dolatti used that accursed globe!"

Kellach, Moyra, and Driskoll looked at each other. "That globe is the reason we're here," Kellach said. "We think it's the key to saving the life of a friend."

"You would risk three lives to save one?" Durmok said. "We should all have such loyal friends."

"Can you tell us where it is?" Driskoll asked.

Durmok grimaced. "I last saw it in the hands of Dolatti, our traps man, but he was the first to fall before the goblins. It may be in their hands now—or perhaps not. Goblins are not known for their ability to appreciate the true value of things. But trust me, you do not want this thing. It is not worthy of your trust."

"You used it?" Kellach asked. "Here, in the dungeons?"

"Yes. The first time, the thing worked perfectly. After that, it was a disaster."

"What happened?"

Durmok smiled at the memory. "When we entered this area, it was infested with all manner of wild creatures, both magical and mundane. We managed to drive most of them off, but some were more stubborn than others.

"The largest of these was a massive owlbear. It was ready to eat us all and pick its beak with our bones. With one sweep of its claws, it knocked me clear across the room. That's how I lost my helmet.

"Before it could strike me with a killing blow, though, Dolatti pointed that gold-banded globe at it and said something strange. The thing tripped over its own feet in the middle of charging at me, and it nearly knocked itself out.

"We scrambled for an exit before it regained its senses, one that was too small for such a monstrous beast to follow through. When it regained its feet, though, it was as if the murder had drained out of it. It was as docile as a kitten. It almost seemed as if it wanted to make friends.

"We weren't ready to cozy up next to the creature, so we moved on. When we left, it cried like an abandoned puppy. It was almost heartbreaking, really.

"Dolatti was thrilled, of course. He thought he had the perfect solution to any fight we found ourselves in. Just direct the globe at whoever was bothering us and *ding!* We had a new friend."

Kellach gasped. "That's not how the globe works at all. Back in Curston, it killed our friend—actually, it set free his soul. We hope to use the globe to recover it."

"I wish you luck," said Durmok. "The thing never seems to work the same way twice. Perhaps it was Dolatti's fault. He only ever knew enough about magic to be dangerous."

"How did he lose the globe?" asked Moyra.

"A little while later, we found ourselves surrounded by goblins. Now, goblins aren't much of a threat to adventurers as seasoned as we, but there were lots of them, a whole town's worth. Dolatti spoke a bit of Goblin, and he persuaded the creatures to take us to their leader, which they did.

"When we finally met the goblin king in his throneroom, he seemed reasonable enough—considering he was determined to have us killed. Well, that's all it took. Dolatti pulled out the globe and aimed it at the king, hoping it would make him our friend. He figured no friend of ours would put us to death.

"It turned out to be the wrong thing to do. The goblin king went insane. He started howling at the top of his lungs, and he grabbed the nearest sword, swinging it at anyone within reach. He killed his queen and his son before anyone really knew what was happening. Then everyone scattered."

"This isn't right," Driskoll said to Kellach. "The first time the globe is used, it kills. The second time, it tames an owlbear. The third time it drives a goblin king mad. Who knows what it might do if we try it on Zendric's corpse?"

"Maybe we're just not thinking about it right," Kellach said, irritated by the implication that they should give up their quest. "Let the man finish his story."

Durmok continued. "In the confusion, Dolatti froze while the crowd swept the rest of us away. The last I saw of him, the goblin king was beating him with the globe. The rest of us managed to escape, but not for long. The goblins blamed us for what had happened—rightfully, of course—and decided we had to pay.

"We thought we could make it back to camp before the goblins caught up with us, but that's when Wencel, our priest, fell into a pit with spikes. With Wencel dead and the goblins closing in on us, we were forced to take off in an uncharted direction. It wasn't long before they caught up with us in this hall.

"I decided to fight a rearguard action at the exit, hoping to give my friends a chance to get out alive. It was their only hope.

"I slaughtered a score of goblins before they finally brought me down. Bleeding from a dozen small wounds, I was left for dead and the goblins continued on after my friends. After they left, I managed to find the strength to crawl along the wall for a ways, hoping to find some other way out of the place. I'd only gotten that far when you charged in with that smoking creature on your tail."

Durmok shifted his weight a bit and winced in pain. "And now that you've healed me, I hope to find a way out of here once again. The goblins may have sated their anger for the moment, but if they find me alive, they are sure to show no mercy."

"May the gods bless your journey," Kellach said.

Driskoll goggled at this. "We're not going with him? Didn't you hear how many goblins are running around down here? In the 'Dungeons of Doom'?"

"The globe is still down here. There's still time. We can still save Zendric."

"Children," Durmok said. "I understand your loyalty to your friend, but—wait. What was his name?"

"Zendric," said Moyra.

Durmok's eyes widened. "Zendric the Gatekeeper? The one who is prophesied to one day renew the seal that was sundered?"

Kellach shrugged. "He's the only Zendric we know."

"If this is the same person, then there is more at stake than simply saving a friend. If he is lost, I have no doubt that this entire region will soon follow. Have no fear." Durmok struggled to his feet and raised his sword. "I will protect—" The sword clattered to the ground as the warrior held his sides in pain.

Kellach rushed to Durmok's side. "You may not be dead, but you're in no condition to do anything other than walk out of here," Kellach said. "You would hinder us more than you could help."

Durmok nodded grimly. "Agreed. I will make my way out as best I can. I believe that the goblin throneroom lies to the north of here." The warrior picked up the sword and leaned on it like a cane.

Kellach pointed toward the passageway he thought headed north. Durmok grabbed the young wizard's hand and turned him a full quarter of a circle. "This way," the warrior said.

"Right." Kellach nodded at the warrior confidently, although he blushed around his collar.

"The goblins are a cowardly lot, but they are agitated. They have lost many of their number today, both to me and my friends and to their own king. If you meet them, be prepared to fight to the last breath."

With that, Durmok limped away. Just before he disappeared into the darkness, he turned and said, "May the gods shine upon your efforts, for if you fail, all may be lost."

13

"Right," Kellach said, turning back to face his friends. "You heard the man. It's up to us to save the day, and time is sailing past. To the north it is." He headed down the hallway.

Both Moyra and Driskoll cleared their throats. Kellach turned back to see why they weren't following, and they pointed in unison to their right and toward the passageway that headed true north. He started to speak, but shut his mouth and struck out again, this time in the proper direction.

After the three friends wandered about for an hour, Driskoll was sure they were lost. "Don't fret about it," Kellach said. "I've been watching. I can find our way back out of here."

"Forgive me if I'm not filled with confidence," Driskoll said.

"What's that supposed to mean?" Kellach asked.

"I think he's saying you'd have a hard time finding your face with a mirror and a map," said Moyra.

"I just—I wish I had a compass. I suppose the two of you think you could do better?" Kellach snapped.

"We could have done at least this well," Driskoll said. "I already know how to get lost."

"Not well enough. I've tried to lose you in Curston dozens of times."

"And you always messed that up too."

"Shut up!"

"Who's going to make me?"

"Would the two of you just be quiet?" Moyra shrieked. "YOU'RE GOING TO GET US CAUGHT!"

Kellach and Driskoll stopped in mid-stride. They stared at Moyra for a moment, then looked at each other and started to laugh. At first they only giggled, but they quickly moved on to full-out belly busters.

"Do you think the Knights of the Silver Dragon ever acted like this?" Driskoll asked.

"I don't know," said Moyra, "but they should have."

Kellach put up a hand to silence them. "Do you hear that?" he whispered.

Driskoll shook his head. "What?"

There it was: a horn sounding in the distance.

"What do you suppose that's for?" Driskoll whispered.

"I don't know," said Kellach. "But it can't be good."

The kids started walking again, and they heard the horn blasting away, over and over. As they moved deeper into the dungeons, the sound of the horn grew closer and closer. At one moment it seemed farther away, and the next it was almost on top of them.

"There's more than one horn!" Kellach said. "They're signaling each other."

"What are they saying?" Driskoll asked.

"I can't tell, but I'd guess it's something like 'Get those noisy kids!' "

The sound of dozens of pattering feet echoed off to the left as the trio came to one of the dungeon's many intersections. Kellach turned to the right and then made a quick left. The kids picked up their pace as the horns sounded behind them. They jogged to their right. The signal behind them seemed to be getting closer.

As the kids rounded a corner, they heard a war cry erupt directly ahead of them, in a language they'd become all too familiar with: Goblin. It wasn't just a single voice but a full chorus of goblin screams that threatened to rattle the stones from the walls.

"Where are they?" Moyra said as they ground to a halt. "Where are their torches?"

Kellach turned around and led the others back the way they had come. "Unlike us, goblins can see in the dark. We won't be able to see them until they're on top of us."

"But they'll be able to see our lantern like a beacon guiding them straight to us," Driskoll said.

Moyra cursed. The horn behind them sounded louder than ever, reminding Driskoll of how some hunters used such noises to drive their prey into a trap. He wondered where the creatures might be sending them, but since their only other choice was to stand and die, he sprinted along behind the others.

The second horn was joined by a third, and it soon became clear that the goblins were surrounding the three friends. With blasts coming from behind them, before them, and to their left, they turned to the right and ran like the Great Seal had been just been sundered and the hordes of the Nine Hells were nipping at their heels.

The kids found themselves in a large room. This one seemed to have once been some kind of auditorium, perhaps a mass meeting hall where the dungeonkeeper could address hundreds of guards at once, back in the days when the city above still thrived. The trio entered at the top tier and raced down the steps to the bottom.

When the kids reached the stage at the base of the room, they realized they were trapped. A large set of double doors stood in the center of the back wall. All three kids tried pulling on the doors at once, but they wouldn't budge. They were locked. The kids hammered on them for a moment, but quickly gave that up.

Moyra crouched in front of the doors and set to examining the lock. Kellach and Driskoll looked around for some other means of escape. But it was too late.

A squad of goblins burst in through the doors in the center of the top tier. Soon after, the doors to the left and right swung wide, and two more squads of well-armed goblins charged in.

When the goblins saw the kids were trapped, they slowed down. With their prey confined, they had time to be cautious, and they were willing to use it. They crept forward, their little swords at the ready. The blades glittered in the lantern light like jewels in the walls of a mine.

The leaders of each of the squads chattered at each other in their guttural tongue. They came forward in unison, making sure that when the final charge came they would not leave a single gap for the kids to exploit.

Suddenly, a booming noise came from the other side of the massive stage doors. Moyra jumped back and nearly fell off the stage. The goblins all halted at the sound, unsure of the source. At first, they seemed to think it was some kind of trick on Moyra's part, but when the sound came again, they knew that couldn't be. It boomed again and then again, now louder.

With the goblins distracted, Moyra prepared to make a break for it. Driskoll knew she couldn't get far. The goblins might have been terrified of whatever was lurking behind that door, but they wanted the kids between them and it.

Kellach stepped up and grabbed Moyra. He whirled her around and spoke directly into her face, softly but as seriously as Driskoll had ever heard him speak. "Can you open that lock?" he asked.

"Why would I want to do something stupid like that?" Moyra asked.

"Answer the question." Kellach looked up and saw that the goblins were starting to inch closer, in spite of the noise behind the door. Some of them seemed to be growing braver, apparently willing to stake their lives on the idea that whatever was behind the door couldn't possibly get through it.

Moyra looked at Kellach as if he were gibbering mad. "That would let the creature behind the door in here!"

"Better that than waiting for goblins to kill us," Kellach said. "The thing on the other side of that door might cause enough of a distraction for us to get away. If it kills us instead, well, we're about to die anyway."

Moyra hesitated, then pulled a set of tools out from her jacket pocket and set to work. Kellach and Driskoll drew their knives and brandished them at the oncoming goblins, who now seemed like spectators gathered around to observe the kids' ultimate fate. Some of the goblins near the upper exits laughed at the boys' efforts, clanging their swords on the benches and stabbing into the air the way they hoped to soon be stabbing into the kids' hearts.

"Got it!" Moyra shouted, then stepped back and held her breath. Both Kellach and Driskoll turned to see what would happen, what kind of beast would hurl itself through the open doors, but all they got was another loud boom as the doors refused to yield again.

"By the gods!" shouted Driskoll, his voice trembling. "How can something that big be so bad at opening a door?"

The goblins nearly fell over themselves laughing. Their relief was palpable, and it spurred them to move even closer. Kellach and Driskoll turned to face them again, and the boys found some of the creatures daring to step within reach of their blades. The brothers made tentative thrusts at the bravest of them. Swords clanked as the goblins' weapons met each feeble blow.

"What should I do?" Moyra asked, nearly hysterical with disappointment.

"It must be latched on the other side!" Kellach shouted over his shoulder. "Use your knife!"

Moyra drew her blade from its sheath on her thigh and waited for the beast to hurl itself against the double doors again. When it did, she shoved the knife into the gap that momentarily formed between the two doors. Her blade wedged there and the creature fell back again.

When the beast pushed against the doors yet again, Moyra shoved the knife in and up. She heard a faint click as the invisible latch flipped out of the way.

The goblins stopped laughing.

The doors burst open, smashing off their hinges as they went. A deafening roar that seemed like it could have knocked the doors off by itself came next, followed by a massive blur of brown fur. It leaped over Moyra, Kellach, and Driskoll and landed amid the stunned goblins.

Three of the goblins were crushed in the initial attack, and the rest turned and fled. They trampled each other on their way up the stairs and out the three exits. One goblin had the sense to blast a sound on his horn that could only have stood for "retreat," but the massive beast swatted him, cutting him off in mid-note.

As the goblins fled, the beast stood up on its hind legs on the stage and unleashed a howl that brought tears to Driskoll's eyes. The younger boy was sure that no goblin would set foot in this room for a long while, if ever.

The beast's head seemed to scrape against the auditorium's vaulted ceiling, but that may have just been a trick of the light. Its thick, dark-brown fur was crusted with the remnants of dozens of meals, most of which consisted of good-sized creatures it had eaten alive. Its arms terminated in massive paws the size of Driskoll's head. Vicious claws sprang from the paws, seeming both longer and sharper than the kids' feeble knives, and red-rimmed eyes glared out at them from above an ivory-tipped beak. The beak looked like it could crack a skull as easily as a bird might open a seed.

It was the creature that had always figured largest in Driskoll's nightmares, the ones that made Driskoll think he'd never fall asleep again. Worse yet, it seemed hungry and mean, and its breath stank like an open grave.

It was an owlbear.

Driskoll screamed his head off.

"Come on!" Moyra pulled Driskoll's arm. They ducked through the now-open double doors, with Kellach right behind.

The kids ran, but as they did, Driskoll knew it was futile. For all its bulk, the owlbear could move with a panther's grace.

The kids found themselves in a wide corridor that led off in two directions. They went right and raced along as fast as their legs would carry them.

Driskoll looked back to see that there was nothing behind them. For a moment, he thought that perhaps he just couldn't see far enough into the dark to find the massive beast, but then he realized that he should have been able to hear its thunderous tread.

"I think it's gone!" Driskoll shouted ahead.

"I don't care," said Moyra, who had somehow found herself in the lead. "I'm not stopping until we're back home. Zendric will have to figure out how to save his soul on his own."

The words had barely left Moyra's mouth when she barreled headlong into a fur-covered wall. She bounced back hard enough to land flat on her back. Her eyes widened as she saw just what it was that she'd run into.

The owlbear was faster than Driskoll had guessed, and it knew the dungeon's maze far better than the kids ever would. It stood there before them, panting out its foul breath as it glared down at them with its crimson eyes.

CHAPTER

14

Everyone froze for a moment, even the owlbear. Driskoll closed his eyes. He didn't want to see what was sure to come next.

Driskoll heard the rumble of the owlbear's panting. He smelled its awful breath. But no shouts. No crunching bones. No screams.

Then Driskoll heard Kellach step forward and say, "Hello."

Driskoll opened his eyes to see his brother walking toward the owlbear. The owlbear watched the apprentice edge forward. Kellach held his arms in front of him, and his fingers trembled.

Then the owlbear reached for Kellach.

"NO!" Driskoll screamed. He launched himself forward, determined to defend his brother with his dying breath.

But before Driskoll could reach them, the owlbear wrapped its arms around Kellach and started to squeeze. Kellach threw his arms wide, in some gesture of helplessness, and squeezed the owlbear back.

Driskoll hurled himself at the owlbear and beat against its arms, but he might as well have been attacking a statue. He screamed at the creature. "Let him go! Let him go!"

It was then that the owlbear loosened its grasp, but only just a bit. Kellach turned toward Driskoll. The younger boy expected to see blood running out of his brother's mouth after the creature had crushed his insides to mush.

Instead, Kellach smiled.

Stunned, Driskoll stepped back. As he did, he tripped over Moyra's legs and fell down next to her.

Driskoll rubbed his eyes and looked again, but the image was still the same.

The owlbear unfurled its arms, and Kellach stepped out of its embrace with a face-splitting grin.

"Don't you get it?" he asked.

Moyra and Driskoll glanced at each other and then back up at Kellach. They slowly shook their heads.

"It's Zendric."

Driskoll was sure the owlbear's hug must have cut off the flow of air to his brother's brain.

"You're cracked," Driskoll said. "Zendric's back in Curston, dead. That—" he pointed up at the creature and realized that his hand was shaking. "That is a vicious, man-eating creature that must have already torn us all apart." Driskoll gasped. "Gods! That's it! I'm dead. This is some sort of death-dream. Something I have to get through before I'm admitted to the afterlife, right?"

Kellach laughed as he walked over and helped both Moyra and Driskoll up. "That's some imagination you have there, but that's not even close to right. We're all alive, and we're all here: you, Moyra, me, and Zendric."

With that last word, Kellach stepped aside and gestured toward the owlbear. Driskoll still wasn't getting it, but neither was Moyra.

"The owlbear ate Zendric?" Moyra asked.

Kellach shook his head and laughed again. "No! Follow me here. Zendric's body is still back in Curston, right where we left it."

Moyra and Driskoll nodded.

"We came here because we're pretty sure Kruncher used that globe to steal his spirit, and the globe ended up here."

The younger two nodded again.

"Well, Zendric's soul is no longer in the globe."

Moyra and Driskoll opened their eyes wide. Kellach pointed back at the owlbear standing behind him, looming over them all, but in a strangely peaceful way.

"Zendric's soul is in there."

Moyra twisted up her mouth. "Kellach, that's the stupidest thing I've ever heard!"

Kellach held up one finger, then turned to the massive beast behind him. It was big enough that its presence actually made the room hotter.

Kellach said, "Zendric?"

The owlbear nodded. As it did, its chest rumbled in a scary way that could only have been its first attempt at laughter.

"This is some kind of trick!" Moyra said. "You used your magic to enslave that beast—or you used it to mess with our minds instead."

"A wizard like Zendric could manage that, true," Kellach said. "But I'm just an apprentice. That's way beyond my command of the powers."

Moyra shook her head as she looked up into the owlbear's red-rimmed eyes. "It can't be," she said. "How?"

Kellach smiled. "You remember the globe we came here for, right? That's how."

Kellach always enjoyed the chance to be a teacher rather than a student, and he threw himself into the role. "The globe—let's call it a 'spiritkeeper,' since that's really what it is. Anyhow, the spiritkeeper is magical device that can be used to steal someone's soul."

"That's what we all thought," Moyra said. "But that's not how it worked for those fortune hunters."

"Right! That's because they didn't understand how it really works. They figured that the spiritkeeper was something like a magic weapon. At first, that's what I thought too, but Durmok's story didn't fit with that at all.

"It's actually a storage device. The soul goes into the globe, and it's preserved there. It's not dead, but without a body, it's not really alive either."

"Which is why we're here," Driskoll said. "If we find the globe, we might be able to free Zendric's soul from it."

"Right! That was the plan, but someone already beat us to it."

Driskoll shook his head, which was starting to hurt. The creature started to tremble then, but Driskoll realized it was trying to laugh without making that terrible sound.

"The adventurers bought the spiritkeeper from Kruncher, right?" said Kellach.

Moyra and Driskoll nodded. The owlbear nodded too.

"They brought it here, and the first time they got into a pinch, they used it—on the owlbear."

"And it sucked its soul away, just like with Zendric," Driskoll said, growing tired of Kellach's game.

Kellach snapped his finger. "Not quite. The spiritkeeper can only hold a single soul at a time."

"So what happens to the other one when—?" Moyra started.

"I get it!" Driskoll shouted. The idea was so explosive, he leaped into the air as it struck him. "When the owlbear's soul went into the spiritkeeper—"

"Zendric's soul went into the owlbear!" Moyra said.

All three of the kids looked up at the owlbear, who nodded sagely at them.

"Gods!" Driskoll said. "This is incredible!"

"And then the fortune hunters used the spiritkeeper on the goblin king," said Moyra.

Kellach nodded. "Which means the goblin king's soul went into the spiritkeeper."

"And the owlbear's soul went into the goblin's body!" Driskoll said.

"So that's why the king seemed to go crazy," Moyra said. "He didn't attack the other goblins. It was the owlbear, who was probably furious to find himself in the king's body."

Then Driskoll looked deep into the owlbear's eyes. "But how do we fix this? I mean, how do we get Zendric out of there and back into his proper body?"

"We still need the spiritkeeper," said Moyra. "If we use it on the owlbear, it will store Zendric's soul again. Then we can run it back to his body in Curston before . . . "

"Before it's too late," Kellach said.

"But—wait a moment," Driskoll said. "What about the goblin king's soul?"

"That would end up in the owlbear, and the owlbear's soul would still be in the goblin king."

"Shouldn't we put them back too?" Driskoll asked.

Kellach's face turned grim. "If we can manage it without either of them trying to kill us on the spot, sure. But that's academic until we find the spiritkeeper. We have to find our way into the goblins' lair and locate the king's throneroom. With any luck, the spiritkeeper is still there."

"Sure," Driskoll said, "along with hundreds of goblins."

"I doubt there are that many of them here in the dungeon," Kellach said. "In any case, we now have a very large advantage in any fight." With that, he looked up at the owlbear, who sat down in front of the kids.

Driskoll stared into the creature's wide, wet, red-flecked orbs. He didn't know for sure what he saw there, but he fancied it was the same amused glint he normally saw sparkling in Zendric's eyes.

"Do you know where we have to go?" Driskoll asked the owlbear.

It nodded, reluctantly, as if it didn't want to show them. A moment later, the massive beast rolled over onto its feet and lumbered off on all fours.

CHAPTER

15

Kellach, Moyra, and Driskoll followed the owlbear deeper and deeper into the dungeons. After only a few minutes, Driskoll was so turned around that he couldn't tell which way was north, much less how they could get back to the exit.

Still, for the first time since the kids had entered the dungeons, Driskoll had a strong hope that they would not only manage to survive but would accomplish what they had set out to do: save Zendric.

From time to time, the owlbear stopped at an intersection of two corridors and raised its head. It sniffed in gallons of air through its humongous beak, sampling the air in each direction. Eventually it came to a decision about which way to go and lumbered off once again.

After moving through one such intersection, the owlbear began to huff and puff louder than ever. It was excited about something for sure.

Then Driskoll heard a horn blast out from the darkness before them. It was clearer and higher than any of the others had been. Almost instantly, answering horn blasts echoed through the corridors. There were so many, it was impossible to tell the number of them and from which directions they came.

The owlbear leaped forward, and the three friends sprinted after it. It seemed to know exactly where they were headed now, although they were running directly into the region from which that first horn had been blown.

Before Driskoll knew what was happening, the owlbear charged into a squad of goblins and sent them flying. Driskoll barely got a look at any of them before the creatures either ran off or were tossed aside. These goblins looked different from the others. They wore rough armor and carried weapons of polished steel. Also, their shields bore some kind of crude heraldry that showed a goblin's head.

If these were the goblin king's elite troops, it made no difference to the owlbear. They might as well have been goblin children instead.

"Stay behind Zendric!" Kellach shouted over the din of the battle. "Keep him between you and the goblins. Some of them have bows, and I don't want any of us picked off by a lucky shot."

In the distance, dozens of horns sounded off. But this time, the high-pitched horn that had started it all failed to answer. Driskoll saw a horn on the ground, and for a moment he thought of picking it up. Before he could see his way clear to the instrument, though, the owlbear stomped on it, crushing it to tiny pieces.

The owlbear lashed all around, letting loose with its horrible howl as it did. In scant moments, the kids found themselves alone with it once again.

Not wasting an instant, the owlbear galloped forward. The kids followed it straight on into the darkness until it skidded to a stop at the end of a hallway. The beast beckoned for them to come around in front of it.

There the kids found a wooden door barred from the outside. Rough carvings on the surface depicted the victory of the goblins in battle with various victims. The central image showed the small creatures swarming over a dragon, stabbing it to death with dozens of blades. If Driskoll had seen such a thing back in Curston, he probably would have laughed. But with the sound of signal horns ringing in his ears, the image shot ice down his back.

Before Driskoll could focus his fears, the owlbear knocked the heavy bar on the door up and over with a flick of its massive paw. Then it tapped the door, smashing it open.

The kids waited for a moment for the creature to lead them into the room beyond. Instead, it sat there and grunted, pointing at the door with a paw.

The owlbear was too big to fit through the doorway. The three friends would have to go through on their own.

Kellach turned to the owlbear and said, "Is this the goblin throneroom?"

The creature grunted loudly and nodded its beaked head.

"Is the goblin king still in there?"

The owlbear did its best to shrug.

Kellach grabbed his pack and drew a torch out of it. He touched it to the fire still burning in his lantern, and it burst into flames.

"This could be dangerous. When we get inside, we'll split up to cover the area faster. You and Moyra stick together."

"Why not split us up too?" Driskoll asked.

"We only have the one torch left," Kellach said as he handed his brother the remaining one. "Now let's move!"

With that, Kellach charged through the door and into the darkness beyond. Moyra and Driskoll chased in behind him and immediately stopped.

The room was even larger than the dining hall where the kids had met Durmok. There was enough space in here for hundreds of goblins to gather. Stone pillars held up the vaulted ceiling high above.

A single shaft of light broke through a carved window in the room's roof, landing squarely on the goblin king's throne. As Driskoll looked up at the window, he realized it was actually a shaft cunningly fitted with mirrors to keep the angle of the light constant as long as there was sun in the sky.

The throne was carved from some kind of red stone. It was tall and wide enough that it would have comfortably fit the owl-bear—had the beast been able to find a way in. In the middle of the seat lay a cushion. It was so large and plush that many goblins could have used it for a bed.

Crimson carpeting ran the length of the hall, from a set of double doors at one end to the throne at the other. The massive doors were closed and had been barred on this side with slabs of timber so large a shipwright could have carved a boat out of them.

The door the kids had come through was in the south side of the hall, about midway between the main doors and the throne. As the three friends entered, Kellach stopped and surveyed the room for a moment. "The place seems empty. The goblin king must have followed the goblins after he chased them all out of here." With that, he immediately struck out for the doors. "I'm going to see if I can figure out a way to let Zendric in."

Moyra and Driskoll headed for the throne. Up close, it was even more impressive. The carvings on the throne had mostly been defaced, but hints of the quality of the artwork were still visible. A massive, gold-crowned goblin head sat atop the throne's high back, looking out over the room's floor beyond.

Moyra and Driskoll mounted the steps of the dais beneath the throne. Moyra leaped up into the seat and snuggled into the cushion. She closed her eyes and held up her face to the sunlight streaming in from above. "Ah," she said, smiling broadly. "It's so warm and bright. I never thought I'd be so happy to see the sun!"

At that moment, Driskoll heard a scratching sound from behind the throne. He poked his nose behind the throne but saw nothing creeping in the darkness.

Driskoll heard Moyra squirming around in her comfortable seat. Then she shouted, "I found it! It was under the cushion!"

Moyra's outburst was the goblin king's cue. Before Driskoll could say a word, the creature climbed over the top of the throne and leaped down on Moyra, screaming incoherently as he fell.

CHAPTER

16

Moyra clutched the spiritkeeper and dived for the floor. The creature landed headfirst on the pillow sitting on the throne. In spite of the cushion, his skull made a loud thump on the stone surface beneath. The impact didn't slow him down for more than a moment. He sprang to his feet, his crown now bent, a gash over his right eye. Standing atop the seat, he let loose a horrible bellow.

From outside the room, the owlbear bellowed in kind, the noise reverberating through the mostly empty chamber until it was almost deafening. The goblin king froze where he stood until the sound died down. For a moment, Driskoll couldn't tell if he was going to explode with fear or frenzy.

Frenzy won.

The goblin king jumped from the seat, clearing all of the steps of the dais and skidded across the floor. Moyra, still holding the spiritkeeper, had been backing slowly away, but as soon as the creature left the throne she sprinted toward the far doors at top speed.

As Driskoll dashed around from the back of the throne, he could see Kellach's lantern bouncing madly back toward them. As far away as his brother was, he still must have heard the goblin king's scream.

Driskoll took off toward the goblin king. Before he could reach the creature, the king spotted Moyra. With a snarl, the king jumped to his feet and gave chase.

Driskoll couldn't believe a creature with such short legs could move so fast. It was all the boy could do to keep up with him, much less make any gains. Still, the creature's rough landing had hurt him a bit, and after a few yards he began limping.

Driskoll put everything he had into a final burst of speed and launched himself at the goblin king's back. The boy wrapped his arms around the king's legs, and they went tumbling.

When the two crashed to a halt, the goblin king landed on Driskoll's chest, knocking the air out of the boy. As Driskoll gasped for air, the goblin king started to hop up and down on his belly, clawing at him with his long, skinny fingers.

Driskoll couldn't help but think that if it had been a real owlbear atop him, he'd already be dead. As it was, the best the scrawny goblin's body could do was make the boy lose his lunch.

When Driskoll finally got the air back in his lungs, he reached up and caught the goblin king in mid-leap. The creature clawed at the boy with his spindly arms, but Driskoll held him out at arm's length, just far enough that the goblin couldn't touch him.

The goblin king turned his head and moved to bite the boy's arm. Before his vicious little teeth could sink home, Driskoll rolled to the side, hurling the creature away as he did. The goblin king tumbled with the impact and bounded back up on his feet.

Driskoll stood up and glared into the goblin king's eyes. The creature inside wasn't used to having anyone stand up to him, having rarely run into someone bigger than him. He was used to fighting smaller foes.

Driskoll was used to fighting his bigger brother. He was ready for the creature now.

The goblin king yowled at the top of his lungs and charged at Driskoll headlong, heedless of his own safety. As an owlbear, the creature would have trampled Driskoll underfoot. Instead, the boy sidestepped him and stuck out his foot. The goblin king tripped right over it and landed square on his face.

Driskoll sprung onto the goblin king and grabbed one of his flailing arms. In one smooth move, the boy wrenched the arm around behind him and put his knee in the creature's back.

"How do you like that?" Driskoll said, leaning down to gloat in the goblin king's ear.

Driskoll was being cocky, and he paid for it. While he was confident he could muscle around the goblin king, he hadn't reckoned on the strength the owlbear's savagery would lend those scrawny arms. He'd forgotten that this wasn't a playground brawl. He was kneeling on someone who was fighting for keeps.

Just as Driskoll finished taunting the goblin king, the creature jerked his head backward. The goblin's skull hit Driskoll square in his nose. Driskoll fell down stunned, blood dribbling from his face. Before he knew what was happening, the creature was on him again, this time trying to rip out the boy's throat with tiny, sharp teeth.

Driskoll managed to get his hands up and around the goblin king's neck. The boy struggled with all his might to push the ferocious creature's face back, but the owlbear spirit in the king was too strong. Those pointy teeth slowly but surely inched closer to the boy's unprotected neck.

Just as Driskoll thought he couldn't hold out any longer, he heard Kellach mutter the strange word on the globe.

A grayish-white glow—like smoke lit from within—enveloped the goblin king, swirling about him like a miniature storm. As it did, the strength left the creature's arms. Driskoll threw him off and scrambled free.

Kellach and Moyra stood nearby, watching the goblin king writhe on the stone floor. Kellach held the spiritkeeper in his hands. Strands of the glowing smoke ran back and forth from it to the goblin king for a long moment. Then they suddenly ceased.

"Amazing," Kellach said under his breath. He looked down at the thing in his hands with a kind of respect Driskoll rarely saw in his eyes.

"I can see why Zendric yelled at you for mishandling that thing," Driskoll said. "But thanks."

Before Kellach could respond, the goblin king stood up. He stared at the throne room around him like he was seeing it with new eyes. Eventually his eyes passed over the three kids, and he nearly jumped out of his orange skin.

The goblin king started for the main doors, but he quickly saw that they were barred. Changing course at top speed, he headed toward the side door the kids had come through instead. As the king got closer, the owlbear stuck his beak through the doorway to see what was going on, and the goblin shrieked.

The goblin king turned to look at the three kids again and spotted the spiritkeeper in Kellach's hands. His face lit up with amazement, followed by a wide and sincere smile. He immediately ran up to them, his arms outstretched.

Driskoll put up his fists, determined to get the best of the goblin king this time around. The creature was faster than Driskoll thought, though, and before the boy knew it the king had his arms wrapped around his chest. For a moment, the boy struggled desperately to get free.

Then Driskoll realized the goblin king wasn't trying to crush him. The creature was hugging him.

The creature let Driskoll go and ran over to embrace Moyra and then Kellach. He squeezed Kellach the longest, babbling something at him in his guttural tongue. Driskoll didn't understand a word of it.

As Kellach managed to work his way out of the goblin king's embrace, he said something to the king in Goblin. This seemed to please the creature even more, as he turned to grin at Moyra and Driskoll, showing all his teeth at once.

"The king," Kellach said, "is grateful to be back in his own body."

"So we gathered," said Moyra, snickering.

"As long as he doesn't attack us again, that's great," Driskoll said. The boy felt his nose. The blood had stopped flowing, but it was still sore.

Kellach finally got a good look at his brother. "Driskoll! I'm sorry I wasn't quicker. Are you all right?"

Moyra stared at the blood that had fallen onto his lips and chin. "I think he's going to live."

Driskoll grabbed his nose and wiggled it, making sure it wasn't broken. "I'll be fine," he said. "Let's just not do that again."

The goblin king stared up at Driskoll with wide eyes. He turned and said something to Kellach. "He's sorry too," Kellach said. "He didn't think he could hurt someone like that."

"Me neither," Driskoll said. "He can make it up to me by showing us the way out of here."

"An excellent idea!" Kellach said. He chattered with the king for a while and then announced. "The king agrees. We'll set out at once."

Kellach, Moyra, and Driskoll started for the side door, but the goblin king balked. "He's afraid of the owlbear," Driskoll said.

Kellach tried to explain the situation to the goblin king, but the creature would have none of it. He seemed sure that they were planning to feed him to the great beast.

Moyra threw her hands up. "If he won't believe you, we'll just have to show him," she said. She walked through the doorway, reached up, and stroked the owlbear's beak.

The goblin king nearly fainted. Once he recovered, he marched straight to the door and stood proudly next to Moyra. He even went so far as to poke the owlbear in the chest. The beast growled at this, but the goblin king refused to cower.

"No goblin male would ever let a female of any kind show him up," Kellach whispered to Driskoll. "Especially not a goblin king."

Kellach and Driskoll hurried to join the others. "Let's go," Kellach said, repeating the request in Goblin. The king proudly took his place at the front of the odd pack and led the way out the side door and down the corridor.

As the group strolled along, Driskoll felt grateful they had the goblin king with them. Without him, the boy was sure that they'd have wandered around the dungeons until some horrible creature ate them or they died of starvation—or both.

A few times, the kids heard horns off in the distance, but the blowers seemed determined to keep their distance. More than once, Driskoll was sure that he heard goblins scurrying around in the darkness. But every time Kellach turned his lantern toward the noises, nothing was there.

Eventually, they reached the exit. The kids tried to say good-bye to the goblin king there, but he insisted on escorting them up into the sunlight. "He claims to be a goblin who pays his debts," said Kellach. "Apparently this is a rare and special trait."

Moyra stifled a cackle, but Driskoll laughed out loud at the sight of natural light pouring down the stairwell. He felt like they had been in the Dungeons of Doom forever, but as he glanced up at the sky, he realized only a few hours had passed. The sun was lowering in the west, but there was plenty of daylight left.

They emerged from the stairwell into the center of the square. The square looked much the same as it had a few hours ago. Directly in front of him, to the east, Driskoll picked out the building in which they'd fought the goblins. From this distance, he could just make out the window in the middle of the vine-covered wall. If the goblin they'd set free hadn't torn down the plants covering it, he was sure he'd never have seen it.

Similar buildings surrounded the once-proud square. Glancing over his shoulder, Driskoll could see the remnant of the clock tower reaching toward the sky, almost as if it were trying to pull free from the vegetation that engulfed it.

The adventurers' campsite was still there, about halfway between the stairs and the edge of the square. The campfire was out now, and it looked even more picked over than before. "I wonder if Durmok made it out?" Driskoll said.

Before anyone could answer, a goblin horn sounded. But this sound did not come from below. It echoed throughout the ruins instead.

At the signal, scores of goblins clambered atop the ruined walls around the square. Many of the orange-skinned creatures bore bows, which they pointed at the group. Others carried only spears or short swords. They were all ready to fight. Even the sight of the owlbear hadn't frightened them off.

"This," Kellach said, "is not good."

CHAPTER

17

The goblin king raised his hands and let loose a shout that rang through the crumbled buildings. For a moment, it seemed as if everyone in the ruins was holding their breath.

Then the goblins unleashed a collective cheer that literally rattled loose some of the surrounding stonework. It was nearly deafening. Even the owlbear cringed at the noise.

At that sound, the king sprinted toward the ruined clock tower, his arms held high in triumph. As the king met the nearest goblins, they wrapped him in a massive hug, happy that whatever had caused his apparent insanity had only been temporary. Another cheer went up from the orange-skinned people.

While many of the king's subjects welcomed him back, the rest kept their attention—as well as their bows—riveted on the owlbear and the kids. No one had shot an arrow yet, but once the cheering was over, they began to chant something in Goblin, over and over.

Driskoll turned to Kellach. The young apprentice looked pale.

"What are they saying?" Driskoll asked.

"Kill them! Eat them! Kill them! Eat them!"

"But the goblin king wouldn't let them do that!" Moyra said. "We saved his life! He's grateful!" Her voice started to trail off. "He wouldn't do that—would he?"

Kellach looked up at the goblin king. His loyal subjects had raised him up on their shoulders and were still cheering at the top of their lungs. Kellach fingered the spiritkeeper nervously and said, "Let's wait and see."

With a single wave of his hand, the king cut off the cheers. A hush fell over the crowd as the goblins all followed their ruler's gaze to where it fell on the kids. In his own tongue, he spoke to the throng of goblins. Kellach translated for Moyra and Driskoll.

"He's thanking his people for their vigilance," Kellach said. "Without them, he never could have survived this ordeal with the white-skinned giants who invaded their home."

"Giants?" Driskoll asked.

"He means us," said Moyra. "Compared to them, we're huge."

Kellach put his finger to his lips. "He swears that he will not allow such a thing to ever happen to his people again." Kellach whispered. "To make sure of this, the invaders will be punished."

"He means Durmok and his friends, right?" Driskoll asked.

As if in answer, every bow pointed at the kids was drawn just a little bit tighter. The sound of creaking bowstrings filled the area.

"Apparently we're close enough," Kellach said.

"You can't do this!" Moyra shrieked at the goblin king. "We saved you!"

Kellach yelled out something in Goblin. Whatever it was set off a murmuring through the crowd. All the goblins looked to their king for a response.

The king rubbed his chin with his long, thin fingers, making sure his subjects knew he was giving full consideration to Kellach's request. After a moment, he leaped down from the shoulders of his followers and marched out to meet the kids.

Kellach and the goblin king spoke quietly for a moment. Eventually, the king threw up his hands and marched back to his followers. As the king scrambled back up onto two goblins' shoulders, Kellach turned to Moyra and Driskoll.

"What was all that?" Driskoll asked.

Kellach gave them a sad smirk. "I tried to convince the goblin king that we were no threat to him."

"We're not," said Moyra.

Kellach nodded. "He didn't care. He said that this was a political matter now. If he is seen backing down to us, his rivals will declare that he is somehow under our control. They'll kill him on the spot, and then kill us for good measure."

"But he's the king! Can't he stand up to them?"

"Sure. Most of the time. But today it looked like he went mad and started killing his own people. His only defense is that the people with the spiritkeeper made him do it." Kellach waved the device for emphasis.

"Why didn't you use that thing on him?" Moyra asked. "That got Durmok and his friends free."

"And mostly dead," Kellach said. "Besides, what do you think will happen if the king suddenly seems to lose his mind again? They'll shoot him dead. The next volley will be for us."

"Why haven't they killed us yet?" Driskoll asked, looking out at the goblins all around. They were murmuring to each other again, but the archers still watched the kids like they were each an angry owlbear.

"The king told me that—out of respect for what we'd done for him—he'd give us a chance to say good-bye to each other. Once I turn around to face him again, his archers will fill us with arrows."

Towering over the kids, the owlbear growled slowly. Kellach reached out and took his paw. The creature calmed down.

The four friends were all quiet for a moment. Driskoll gritted his teeth to hold back the tears of frustration in his eyes. Moyra's eyes shone with uncowed anger.

"I shouldn't even mention this," Kellach said, "but you have the right to know." He took a deep breath and looked out over the crowd of goblins before he spoke again.

"The king offered me—us—a deal. He's willing to let us go if we give him something."

"What?" Driskoll asked.

Kellach held up the spiritkeeper once again.

"If we give him this, he'll let us go." Kellach looked up at the owlbear again. "But not all of us."

Driskoll looked at both Moyra and Kellach, then up at the owlbear. Moyra shook her head from side to side, her red hair swaying with her. The look of determination never left her face. Kellach's blue eyes were clear and strong, but troubled. The owlbear huffed and puffed as if he was ready for a fight.

"I say we put it to a vote," Driskoll said. Moyra and Kellach nodded their approval. The owlbear made a curious sound in the back of its throat and watched.

"All in favor of giving the goblin king what he wants?"

No one raised a hand. The kids all smiled at each other. The owlbear seemed to chuckle a bit.

"That's settled," Driskoll said, "but now what do we do?" He couldn't keep a tremor from his voice. He wasn't looking forward to the answer.

Kellach was silent for a moment. He hefted the spiritkeeper in his hand and peered into its smoky depths as if it were some kind of crystal ball that would give up the answers they needed. The kids all looked at it for a moment. The only thing that filled Driskoll's head was the thought that they would all soon die.

Then Kellach looked up at the others and smiled. "I have a plan."

After a few hurried whispers, the kids and the owlbear were ready. The goblin king called out to them.

"He wants to know if we've made our peace with the gods," Kellach said, grinning.

"Is this going to work?" Driskoll asked.

Kellach shrugged. "There's only one way to find out."

With that, the three kids walked around behind the owlbear, who got down on all fours and then lay flat on the ground. Even then, the beast was still taller than any of them.

Moyra started to cry at the top of her lungs. Driskoll followed right after her. They hugged each other, huddled down behind the owlbear, and wailed, making as big a scene as they could.

Meanwhile, Kellach whispered the word to the spiritkeeper. That same grayish-white glow erupted from the device and enveloped the owlbear, swirling about its body like a tornado. The creature started to shake.

For a moment, the goblins didn't know what to think. The archers nervously stretched their bowstrings as far back as they would go. A hush fell over the rest of the crowd. The silence was finally broken by the goblin king's laughter. The king shouted something and pointed at the owlbear. The whole crowd began laughing too.

"The king thinks we goofed," Kellach said, grimly. "He thinks I'm attacking the owlbear."

"Are you done yet?" Driskoll whispered. He and Moyra had given up the weeping and wailing.

The last wisps of the mist between the owlbear and the spirit-keeper parted, melting into the warm air. The great beast stretched its limbs for a moment, as if it had just awakened from a long sleep. It turned its head from side to side, taking in the scene of scores of goblins surrounding it, weapons at the ready. Then its eyes settled on the goblin king, sitting on his followers' shoulders.

The owlbear suddenly sprang up to its full height and unleashed a sky-shattering roar.

Kellach looked at Driskoll with wide eyes and whispered, "Oh, yeah. We're done."

The owlbear came down on all fours with enough force to shake the ground under the kids' feet. The goblins surrounding the square gasped with fear. Before they could react, the monster sprinted toward the king and his contingent.

"Now!" Kellach whispered to Moyra and Driskoll as he grabbed their shoulders and pushed them ahead of him.

The goblin archers let loose a hail of their black arrows at the owlbear. A good number of them found their mark, but just as many sailed past and into the goblins around the king.

The king squealed something at the archers. Before he could finish, though, his followers dropped him from their shoulders and ran.

Driskoll didn't see what happened after that. He was too busy running for his life.

CHAPTER

18

Kellach, Moyra, and Driskoll didn't stop running until the ruins were far behind them. Eventually, they threw themselves into a stand of trees by the side of the road, entirely out of breath.

It was a long moment before any of them could say anything. Once Driskoll had caught his breath, he lay there for a moment listening as intently as he could.

Moyra panted, and Kellach was still gulping for air. Birds chirped in the trees. Driskoll heard his own heart beating in his ears.

But Driskoll didn't hear anything that sounded like a pack of angry goblins chasing after them. Nor was there a mad owlbear rampaging down the road. It seemed that the kids had gotten away.

Driskoll started to laugh, softly at first, as he was still a little out of breath. Moyra joined in right away, and Kellach pitched in soon after. Their chuckles gradually grew to flat-out roars.

"Did you see the look on the king's face?" Moyra said. "Priceless!"

"That poor owlbear!" said Kellach. "Can you imagine? One minute you're facing down a group of adventurers in your lair, and the next thing you know you're out in the sunlight, surrounded by goblins!"

Driskoll laughed until his belly hurt more than his legs. Then he laughed some more. They all did.

"It's getting dark," Moyra said. "We'd better get going."

Kellach stood up and helped her to her feet. "We have less time than you might think," he said, finally taking the time to store the spiritkeeper in his pack. "To be certain that we can help Zendric, we need to get his soul back into his body before a full day has passed."

Driskoll bounded to his feet. "And if we don't?"

Kellach shook his head. "I don't know. I'd rather not find out."

With that, the kids set off for Curston once again. They walked at a stiff pace, just shy of a run.

As the sun finally fell behind the hills, the gates of Curston came into sight. The three friends trotted along for the last bit, not saying a word, but grinning at each other like fools. They were alive, they had saved Zendric's soul, and they were proud of it.

When the kids got to the Westgate, it was already closed for the night. They dashed the last hundred yards up to the tall, ironbound doors and banged on them with all their might. For a long while, nobody inside paid any attention. Then a watcher stuck his head out over the battlements on the top of the wall above the gate.

"The town is closed for the night!" the watcher shouted down. "You'll have to wait until morning!"

"We can't wait that long!" Moyra shouted back. "This is an emergency! Let us in!"

The watcher goggled at them for a moment, then turned to talk with someone standing next to him. "By the gods," he said, "they're children."

The watcher stuck his head back out over the wall's edge. "I'm sorry, young ones," he said, "but I can't open the gates. They're locked, and the keyman won't return until dawn breaks."

"What's your name?" Kellach shouted up.

The watcher squinted at the trio in the dimness. "That's none of your concern," he said. "I'll not be giving out my name to any creatures outside the walls after dusk, no matter what shape they might take."

"He thinks we're monsters," Driskoll said. "That we're trying to trick him."

"It's happened before," Kellach said. "More than once. There are reasons for those rules."

"We have to get inside!" Moyra said, almost screeching. "I don't want to be out here all night with the real monsters!"

"Hold on a moment," Kellach said, scratching his chin as he looked up at the gates. "I'll think of something."

The three friends waited there for a few long moments, the last rays of light dying in the sky behind them. Kellach opened his mouth to speak, but before he could the watcher appeared above the wall again. "This is your lucky day!" he shouted down. "Stand back! We have someone leaving the city!"

Driskoll looked at Kellach. "No one leaves Curston at night," Driskoll said. "It's suicide."

"Don't turn up your nose at good fortune," Moyra said.

Kellach nodded in agreement.

A clanking sound rang behind the Westgate as the massive lock on the bars was removed. Then metal scraped on metal as a team of watchers drew back the three gigantic, ironbound logs that barred the gate at night. By the time the doors swung open, Driskoll realized he was holding his breath in anticipation.

A team of horsemen galloped out through the doors as soon as there was enough room. The horses were terrified by the darkness falling on the land—and what might be in it—but they obeyed their riders' commands. The animals thundered out through the gate and before the kids knew what was happening, armored riders, their swords drawn and ready, surrounded the three friends.

"Hold!" a voice called out. Kellach, Moyra, and Driskoll threw up their hands, doing their best to seem as harmless as possible.

One of the horsemen leaped from his saddle and landed right before them. He wore a full suit of chainmail and bore a shield with the crest of Curston emblazoned across it. The golden trim that ran around its edge declared him the captain of the watch.

It was Torin. He gathered up his sons and their friend in a massive embrace.

"Moyra! Boys!" he said. "By the gods, I feared you were all dead. Are you unharmed?"

All three of the kids nodded. "Good," Torin said as his mood turned foul, "because you're in a lot of trouble."

The kids tried to explain themselves, but every time they opened their mouths, Torin shouted them down. "I might have expected a stunt like this from Moyra—considering her father's influence—but you two have truly disappointed me," Torin said to his sons. He had three of his men put the kids before them on their horses, and he led them through the streets of Curston to his home.

As the group rode through the gate, the doors shut behind the riders, and the bars were pushed back into place. It was past curfew and the city streets were almost entirely abandoned, barring the occasional watcher.

Driskoll tried to talk to Kalmbur, who carried him on his horse, but the elf refused to listen to the boy or even make eye contact. To do so would have brought Torin's wrath down on the watcher too, and Kalmbur was far too clever to risk that needlessly.

When the riders reached the house, Torin dismounted and ordered his watchers to bring the kids inside and deposit them in the front parlor. The watchers did so wordlessly, each refusing to make eye contact with the kids. Many of them had tasted Torin's anger in the past, and they knew it would only make things worse if they were to speak in the kids' defense.

The other watchers departed, leaving Kellach, Moyra, and Driskoll sitting in the chairs facing the hearth. Torin stood before the cold and empty fireplace and spoke. His words were hard, but his tone was far worse.

"After spending hours rounding up suspects in Zendric's murder and putting them through various tests, I get word that the three of you were spotted wandering around the prison without an escort. I come home to check up on you, and what do I find?" Torin asked.

Driskoll started to answer, but Torin cut him off. "Nothing! No sons anywhere. 'It's been a rough day on them,' I tell myself. 'Be kind. The incident in the prison was probably a harmless prank.'

"This lasts until I get word from the Westgate that a renowned warrior called Durmok has just staggered in from the ruins."

"Durmok? Is he all right?" Moyra asked.

"You admit to knowing him?" Torin growled. Moyra could only nod.

"We took Durmok to the Hall of Healing straight away. He was badly hurt, but he'll survive. Fortunately, he was well enough to be questioned."

Torin gritted his teeth. "This Durmok told me that he and his companions had met an ill fate in the ruins."

"In the Dungeons of Doom," Driskoll said.

Torin's face lit up with fury. "Where did you hear that name?" he asked through a clenched jaw.

Driskoll melted in the heat of Torin's anger. "Durmok," he said weakly.

"You are never to repeat that," Torin said. "Never. This city has come far since the Sundering of the Seal, and I'll not have my own sons stirring up interest in a dangerous place far better left alone!"

Driskoll nodded apologetically.

"And no more interruptions. Keep silent until I finish."

All three of the friends nodded.

"Durmok reported that he had discovered three children—by the names of Kellach, Driskoll, and Moyra—wandering around in the dungeons. He said that you saved his life there, but that you insisted on continuing on through the place rather than accompanying him back to Curston."

The kids all opened their mouths to protest this, but Torin's glare shut them up.

"I rarely trust the word of a fortune hunter, but the fact that he had all three of your names could not be ignored. I rounded up my best watchers to mount a rescue, despite the late hour.

"Do you understand? I was going to risk the lives of my best people, not to mention my own life, to rescue you. You not only put yourselves in danger but all of those fine people too. Now tell me. What in the gods' secret names were you thinking? And this had better be good."

Moyra and Driskoll both looked at Kellach. He might have been trembling, but he steeled himself and spoke.

"We figured out that a half-orc named Kruncher had stolen Zendric's soul," Kellach began.

"That petty thief?" Torin asked. "You expect me to believe he has the brains to take on Zendric?"

"That's not what I said. If you'll let me finish . . ." Kellach waited for a moment until Torin nodded for him to go on.

"Kruncher used one of Zendric's own devices to capture Zendric's soul. Then he sold it to Durmok and his friends. We had to go into the dungeons after them to get it back."

Torin stared at Kellach for a moment before he spoke.

"Kellach, I know you're a bright boy. Barring your mother, you're the smartest person I've ever known. But you don't have the common sense the gods gave a rock."

"But, Dad," Kellach started.

"Don't 'but, Dad,' me! This Kruncher is a known con artist. You boys had a run-in with him just last night. And you were dumb enough to believe him when he spun a story that ended with you needing to go into the Dungeons of Doom? There's nothing more to say. He hoodwinked you, and you all nearly died because of it."

"But Dad," Kellach said, "we found it. We found the spirit-keeper!"

Torin wouldn't believe a word of it. "So you found some bauble in the dungeons. The place is filled with such things, and none of them have anything to do with Zendric's missing soul."

"Dad," Kellach said, doing his best to remain calm, "we need to bring this device to Zendric's body so we can restore his soul to him. And we need to do it now."

"You're not going anywhere, young man," Torin said. "Until further notice, you and your brother are both confined to quarters. If I catch you so much as tiptoeing outside of this house, I swear on St. Cuthbert's holy cudgel I'll toss you in the prison for a week!"

"But, Dad!"

"And you can put this foolishness out of your head right now. Zendric is dead. Lexos pronounced him so this afternoon."

Kellach had been edging forward in his seat, but this news sat him back, stunned. "Are you sure?" he asked quietly. "Maybe there's still time."

"There is not," said Torin. "The wizard's body is resting in the House of the Dead. It'll be incinerated in the morning, and you can put all this out of your mind."

"Dad, no!" Kellach shouted. "You can't do that. I have to see him. There could still be time."

"Forget it," said Torin. "It's after dark. You're not going any- where." He shook his head. "I've had enough of this. This has been a horrible day. The lot of you are going to sleep. We'll talk about this again in the morning."

"What about me?" asked Moyra.

"It's too late to bring you home now," Torin said. "You can take my bed upstairs, in the room next to the boys'. I'll lie on the cot down here."

"But my mother will worry," said Moyra.

"No more than usual," said Torin. "You've been out all night before, Moyra. I took your mother's complaints personally." He shook his head sadly. "I remember the three of you playing as kids. You had such promise."

Driskoll started to say something, but Torin cut him off. "No more, son. To bed with you all. Now." He pointed the kids up the stairs, and they filed off silently and dejected.

CHAPTER

19

"How could he not believe us?" Driskoll asked as he and Kellach walked into their room and shut the door.

"It's not that he didn't believe us," said Kellach. "He didn't even listen to us. If he had, then he'd have had the chance not to believe us. He didn't even get that far."

"So what do we do now?" Driskoll asked. "We can't just sit here and do nothing."

"Of course not. But we need to take care of a few details before we leave." Kellach was busy bundling spare clothes into his bed to make it look as if he were sleeping under his heavy woolen blanket. Driskoll immediately set about doing the same for himself.

Just as the boys finished up, they heard a light tap at the door. Kellach went over to open it, and Moyra slipped in.

"Thank the gods you're still up," Moyra said. "I knew you two wouldn't give up that easily."

"Is he asleep yet?" Kellach asked.

Moyra shook her head. "No. He's down there, pacing in front of the fire, muttering to himself."

"Can we wait for him to nod off?" Driskoll asked. "Do we—I mean, does Zendric have that kind of time?"

Kellach pulled the spiritkeeper out of his pack and stared at it. "He should," he said, "but I wouldn't want to push it. There's no telling how being in that owlbear might have affected him. A soul's not meant to be in a body other than its own."

"Then we'll just have to go out the window," Moyra said.

"We're a good twenty feet up," Driskoll said. "I don't think we can jump that far."

Moyra turned to Kellach. "You still have that rope in your pack, don't you?"

"Right!" said Kellach. "We can just shimmy down it and be on our way."

∎ ∎ ∎ ∎ ∎

It wasn't quite that simple, but it worked out in the end. Moyra tied the rope to the leg of Driskoll's bed, and the boys lowered themselves down it one by one. Driskoll went first, then Kellach. Moyra untied the rope and slung it over her shoulder. As the best climber, she scaled down the rough-sided building until she was close enough to street level to jump.

It was then that Driskoll realized they were out on the streets of Curston after dark, by themselves. This was the one thing Torin had hammered into his sons' heads that they absolutely could not do, ever since the Sundering of the Seal. Torin regularly came home with horrible stories about people who'd been wandering about the streets of Curston after dark and had been torn to bits by one sort of supernatural creature or another.

The three friends stole through the city streets like ghosts. Lampposts stood on every street corner. Candles shone in many windows, a tiny charm devised by the superstitious to keep monsters at bay.

Three blocks from the boys' home, the lights came to an end. The buildings turned from homes to shops. These were mostly abandoned after dusk, their owners returning to them at the first hint of daybreak. No candles burned in these windows. Bars of cold iron protected them instead.

A howl pierced the silence, like a siren floating above the city's rooftops. It sounded like a dozen angry dogs yowling in unison, their voices melding to form a single, terrifying scream.

"Wh-what was that?" Driskoll asked. He slapped a hand over his own mouth when he heard how loud he sounded.

"Just keep moving," Moyra whispered, "and pray you never find out."

The trio moved along more quickly now. The creature out there—whatever it was—let loose with another howl, somewhere off to the right. It was closer this time.

"Maybe we should turn back," Driskoll whispered.

"We can't let Zendric die," Kellach said.

Another vein-chilling howl breached the night. This time, it came from directly behind them.

The kids froze and listened. For a long moment, the only thing they heard was their own measured breaths and their hammering hearts. Then, from the blackness behind them came the sound of a predator's clawed feet tapping against the cobblestone paving. It continued for a minute, then stopped short, still well out of sight.

"Main Square is only a few blocks from here. It's lit all night long," Kellach said evenly. He'd given up on whispering. "When I say go—"

Kellach never had the chance to finish.

A massive beast emerged from the shadows. It was shaped like an enormous dog, but far more vicious and well muscled than any mutt Driskoll had ever seen trotting through the streets of Curston. It seemed to be composed almost entirely of darkness itself. The only bits of it that showed any color were its blood-red tongue, its sharp, white teeth, and its glaring eyes, which glowed like the embers of a fire.

Without a word, Kellach, Moyra, and Driskoll turned and sprinted, the creature hot on their heels.

"Hurry!" Moyra shouted. "Don't look back! Just run!"

Moyra charged ahead into the maze of booths that littered Main Square. Unlike the streets leading up to Main Square, the square itself was bathed in light. To keep away the creatures that terrorized Curston at night, the merchants had invested in scores of everburning torches. At least one was mounted over the front of each stall, illuminating the place throughout the darkest hours.

Although the boys could barely see Moyra, running far ahead of them, Driskoll kept them on her trail.

"How do you know which way to go?" Kellach asked.

"She's heading for the obelisk," Driskoll said. As the boys turned along another row of permanent booths, Driskoll pointed up at the marble needle that towered over the stalls, marking the exact center of the square.

Driskoll glanced over his shoulder. He didn't see the creature any longer, but he could hear its howls. "I thought it would have caught us by now," he said.

"It doesn't like the light," said Kellach. "The creature doesn't trust it."

"Then it's really not going to like this," Driskoll said. The two brothers burst from the labyrinth of booths into the center of the plaza.

Even in the spare moonlight, the white obelisk shone like a beacon in the night. The sundial etched in the pavement around it seemed as bright as day. As the boys sped toward the circle of runes, they saw Moyra standing next to the obelisk. She shaded her eyes as she scanned the many entrances from the maze of booths, hoping to see her friends. When they crossed over the edge of the sundial, she let out a little cheer and waved for them to join her.

"I thought I'd lost you," Moyra said as the boys raced to meet her.

"Not a chance," Kellach grinned.

Driskoll stared at them both. "I don't understand what you two are so happy about. We still have that monster chasing us!"

Kellach shook his head. "We're safe here." He pointed back to the way they'd come. "Look."

Driskoll turned to see the beast emerge from the maze of booths. It came directly up to the edge of the sundial's circle and then paced alongside it, moving back and forth like a caged tiger.

"I don't get it," he said. "What's stopping it?"

Kellach pointed to the runes etched along the sundial's rim. "You see those markings? The entire sundial is a massive ward,

147

a circle of protection against the kinds of creatures that roam Curston at night."

"Amazing," Driskoll said, then shook his head. "Why don't they just surround the entire city in one of these?"

"They don't normally work on a large scale," said Kellach. "Too many things can go wrong. This is the largest one I've ever heard about."

Driskoll turned to Moyra. "Am I the only one who didn't know about this?"

Moyra shook her head. "I was just waiting here for you two to catch up."

"Only the watch and those on the ruling council know about this," Kellach said. "I recognized the writings one day and asked Zendric about it directly. He said they didn't want to give anyone a false sense of security about breaking curfew."

"This is great!" said Driskoll. "We're perfectly safe. All we have to do is wait until morning, and the monster will go away, right?"

Kellach grimaced. "We don't have that long."

As if to punctuate the statement, the beast pacing the edge of the circle let loose with a howl so horrifying that Driskoll found himself clinging to his older brother. When the moment passed, Kellach squirmed out of the embarrassed Driskoll's grasp.

"There's no time to lose," Kellach said. He reached into his pack and rummaged around for a few moments. He pulled out a handful of small, leather pouches and picked through them until he found the right one.

"You'd better have something pretty incredible up your sleeve this time," Moyra said to the apprentice, who still had his nose in his pack.

"Why's that?" Kellach said absentmindedly, concentrating on the task at hand.

"The monster's got friends."

Kellach looked up to see that five more shadowy creatures had joined the beast. Each of them looked just as vicious, hungry, and evil. They were the perfect predators, and now they had a full pack.

"That does complicate things a bit," Kellach said. He put his pack back in order and opened the pouch he'd chosen. "But it doesn't change the plan. Get ready, you two. This is going to happen fast."

Kellach began to chant, his voice steady and even. As he spoke, he reached into the pouch and pulled out a white hair. He swung the hair through the air in an intricate pattern, and just as he finished chanting, he flicked it away.

In the blink of an eye, the hair disappeared, and an ivory-colored stallion stood in its place. There was a handsome leather saddle atop its back and a bit already in its mouth. The bridle hung down to where Kellach could grab it. The animal's eyes instantly grew wide as it took in the scene around it. Before it could panic, Kellach snatched up the horse's reins and held them tight.

"Climb on!" Kellach said to Moyra and Driskoll. "We'll have to squeeze."

Kellach hopped up into the saddle and pulled Moyra up behind him. Driskoll scrambled up after her, riding bareback. The beasts outside the circle started to growl in unison.

Kellach turned the horse toward the direction from which the kids had entered the square. The monsters nearly collided as they raced to form a giant snarling pack in front of them. Still safe in

the protective circle, Kellach held the reins tight, letting the horse dance before the pack, almost teasing the beasts.

Then, without warning, the horse spun and galloped off in the other direction at top speed. Driskoll whooped as the animal burst out of the circle's protection and headed off into the dark streets of Curston. As fast as they were moving, he didn't think anything could ever catch them.

As the three friends neared their destination, Kellach pulled up on the reins, and the horse ground to a stop. "We walk from here," he said. "The watchers guarding the House of the Dead would shoot the horse on sight."

Driskoll reached out and stroked the horse's coat. "What will happen to him?" he asked.

"He saved our lives," said Moyra. "We can't just let those beasts find him wandering the streets."

Kellach turned to the horse and patted him on his neck. "You have served us well, friend. Go in peace." With that, the horse disappeared, leaving not even a tuft of hair in its place.

"Now," said Kellach as he turned toward the others, "it's time to save Zendric."

CHAPTER

20

The House of the Dead was a foreboding stone structure. Watchers stood guard around the clock, and the streets on all sides of the place were lit up with dozens of torches.

In the torchlight, the flickering shadows made the façade of the House of the Dead seem to come to life. The stone front was covered with carvings that depicted the gods escorting their believers into the afterlife. Statues of skeletons of all kinds—human, dwarf, elf, halfling, gnome, and some Driskoll couldn't identify—framed the place on every side. Their empty eye sockets all seemed to watch the kids as they crept toward the place.

A pair of watchers flanked the front doors. They were somber and serious, staring out into the night for the slightest sign of trouble. A second pair of watchers strolled around the building in one direction, patrolling the perimeter. Only moments later, another patrol came around from the other direction.

"How are we going to get in there?" Driskoll asked. "That place is sealed up tighter than the city treasury."

"I know how to handle this, boys," Moyra said. "Follow my lead."

Before Kellach or Driskoll could stop her, Moyra strode forward into the open square in front of the House of the Dead. The watchers instantly snapped to attention, all their focus now on her—and on the brothers as they trotted up behind her.

"Hold!" one of the watchers shouted. "You are in violation of the town curfew. Stand where you are!"

Moyra began wailing loudly and then fell to her knees and crumpled up into a sobbing heap. Kellach and Driskoll caught up with her. They kneeled down behind her to comfort her.

"What's wrong?" Driskoll asked.

"Nothing," Kellach whispered as Moyra wailed even louder. "Play along."

"It's okay," Driskoll said loudly. "It'll be all right."

"No, it won't!" Moyra said between sobs. "My father is dead!"

Driskoll looked up at the guards and saw them flash each other knowing looks. A watcher walked forward and stood over them. He waited patiently until Moyra calmed herself and then he spoke.

"Who is your father?" the watcher asked. He did not appear to be bothered by Moyra's tears.

"B-Breddo," Moyra said. "His name is Breddo. He was in the prison, but they said he was murdered there this evening."

The watcher nodded. "If that's true, then he'll be inside already. Come with me."

The three kids stood up and followed the watcher to the entrance. The doors were locked, but they opened silently, on well-oiled hinges, at a knock and password from the watcher.

Once the kids were all inside, the watcher turned around to get a good look at them. Until that point, Kellach and Driskoll had tried to avoid his eyes, but now that was impossible.

"Hold," the watcher said. "I recognize you boys. You're Torin's sons, right?"

The brothers nodded. Driskoll's heart beat so hard he thought the watcher might be able to see it through his shirt.

"What are you doing out tonight with this girl? You should know better than to break curfew."

"She's a family friend," Kellach said. "She came to us and told us her horrible news, then declared she was coming here. We couldn't let her walk the city streets alone." As he spoke, Moyra began sobbing again.

"You couldn't stop her?" the watcher asked.

With that, Moyra let loose a wail that echoed down every hallway in the House of the Dead. Kellach and Driskoll looked at the watcher helplessly and shrugged. He nodded with a grimace, then gestured to the boys to comfort her again.

The brothers patted Moyra on the back and held her until her cries subsided. When they looked up again, someone had joined the watcher. The torches behind the person cast him in shadow, so Driskoll didn't recognize him at first. When the newcomer spoke, though, Driskoll had no doubt who it was.

"Thank you, watcher," said Magistrate Lexos. "I'll take it from here."

The watcher nodded to the magistrate and immediately returned to his post, leaving Kellach, Moyra, and Driskoll alone with Lexos in the foyer of the House of the Dead. The magistrate was dressed in the black version of his robes of office, the ones he wore during funerals and other somber affairs. These bore the insignia of St. Cuthbert as well.

Lexos moved so that his face was now in the light, and the kids could see the concern in his eyes. "Children," he said softly, "what seems to be the matter?"

Kellach, Moyra, and Driskoll all stared up at the priest wordlessly, their mouths agape.

"We came to see Zendric," Driskoll said. For that, he got Kellach's elbow between the ribs.

"Do you mind if we pay our last respects?" Kellach said.

"Actually, yes," Lexos said. "We have a strict policy against disturbing the bodies at night. If you wish, you may say your prayers over him tomorrow. We will have a quick ceremony upstairs just after dawn."

"But we can't wait that long," said Driskoll. Kellach's elbow seemed even sharper this time.

"He can tell if we're lying," Driskoll whispered to Kellach. "Maybe he can help us."

"Exactly how can I help you?" the magistrate said.

Lexos pursed his lips as he stared at the three friends, sizing them up like produce in the city market. Moyra smiled warmly at him, and Kellach nodded his assent.

"We need to see Zendric's body," Driskoll said. "We think we can save him."

Lexos arched an eyebrow at that. "Despite my best efforts, my son, I was not able to help poor Zendric. With his soul departed, he remains beyond my help."

"But we can restore his soul to him," said Driskoll. He turned to Kellach. "Go on, show him."

Lexos watched as Kellach reached into his pack and pulled out the spiritkeeper. His face remained unperturbed. "This device could restore Zendric to life?"

The three friends nodded.

Lexos reached out and took the spiritkeeper from Kellach. He turned it slowly in his hands, examining the runes. "I've seen this before," he said. "On Zendric's mantel, I believe."

"That's right," said Driskoll.

"How did it come into your possession?" the magistrate asked as he returned the device to Kellach.

"That's an all-day story," said Kellach. "We need to get to Zendric soon, or we may be too late to do him any good."

The magistrate hesitated for a moment, then nodded. "All right, children. Follow me."

Lexos turned and walked over to a side door in the right wall of the foyer. He held it open for the kids and watched them file past him one at a time. Beyond the door, a stairwell led down to a long hallway lined with everburning torches.

At the bottom of the stairs, the kids waited for Lexos to take his place before them again. They followed the magistrate through a maze of corridors. As they walked, he spoke. "Have you ever been down here before, children?"

Kellach, Driskoll, and Moyra shook their heads.

"This is where we hold the dead for the requisite three days before their mandatory cremation. Family and friends may visit during that time, and we usually hold a memorial service in the church upstairs, unless the deceased or his survivors request otherwise."

"Three days? I hear that you're planning to cremate Zendric tomorrow," Kellach said.

"Who told—ah, yes. Your father would know that." Lexos frowned. "For Zendric, we've decided to make a special exception. He is clearly dead and beyond the means of even the most powerful priest to aid. What's more, there is the worry that a rogue spirit could somehow possess a wizard of such power and bend Zendric's talents to its needs. That's a risk we'd rather not take."

"But if we can restore his soul?" Kellach asked. "Won't he be just fine then?"

Lexos shook his head as he walked. "One can only hope. But reuniting body and soul is always a tricky proposition, boy, especially when they've been forcibly separated like this. We have no way of knowing if that device of yours will work."

Just then, Lexos came to a halt before a stone door that bore a heavy lock. "Zendric is in here," he said. "This is one of our cremation chambers."

"How many do you have?" Kellach asked.

"Two. The other is empty."

With that, the magistrate withdrew a key from his robes and undid the lock. Then he slid open the door to the room and gestured for the kids to precede him inside.

The cremation chamber was dark, but Lexos had taken a torch from outside the door and brought it with him. The room was small, cramped even, with a ceiling that nearly brushed the top of Lexos's head. It was bare except for three slabs of stone, each standing atop a thick pedestal in the center of the room.

A body lay on the central slab, covered head to toe with a long white sheet. The linen was too thick to see through, especially in the dim light. With the kind of day the kids had endured,

Driskoll didn't know if he would have been surprised if Zendric suddenly sat up beneath the cloth and laughed.

"You may try your device if you like," Lexos said to Kellach. "I can see that you have high hopes pinned on your attempt, although I do not expect it to work. Zendric's soul has long since left us."

Kellach drew the spiritkeeper from his pack again. The smoke inside it swirled faster than ever, agitating against the interior of the globe as if it wanted to break free. Kellach pointed the device at the corpse on the table and muttered the magic word.

Nothing happened. The smoke inside the globe whirled for a moment, but it quickly slowed down again. No ghostly smoke erupted from it, and the corpse on the table didn't budge an inch.

"Something's wrong," said Driskoll. "It should work."

"Maybe you didn't do it right," Moyra said to Kellach.

"No," Kellach said. "Something's not right. This is simple to use."

Lexos muttered, "Even a half-orc thug could manage it."

Kellach's jaw dropped. "How did you know a half-orc used it?"

Lexos's face turned stony. It was a moment before he replied. "I was just offering an example. I could just as easily have said 'a half-witted apprentice.' "

"But you didn't," said Kellach. "You said 'half-orc thug.' Why a thug?"

"Aren't all half-orcs thugs?" Lexos smirked as he looked down at the kids.

"You're lying," Kellach said.

The magistrate laughed coldly. "What are you talking about, boy?"

"It all adds up." Kellach stared hard into Lexos's eyes. "It was you. You killed Zendric."

Moyra and Driskoll gasped and stared at both Kellach and Lexos. The apprentice and the priest regarded each other with hard looks filled with disgust and hate. Driskoll grabbed Moyra's arm and pulled her backward, putting the stone table between them and the others.

"You're stricken with grief for your teacher, boy," Lexos finally said. "You've let your imagination run away with you."

"You let your ambitions run away with you," Kellach said.

"I thought Kruncher killed Zendric," Driskoll said.

Kellach never took his eyes off Lexos. "You hired Kruncher to handle your dirty work for you."

"I never hired anyone," Lexos said angrily, "especially not some dirty half-orc thief! You had best watch your tongue, boy, before it lands you in more trouble than it can talk you out of. I'll not be so merciful in my judgment this time."

"Technically, you're right," Kellach said. "You never 'hired' Kruncher. You made a deal for his cooperation. Kill a wizard and be set free."

"He gave up his hand for his freedom," Lexos said. "I saw the punisher take it with his axe."

"And you restored it to him that night," Kellach said, with each word stabbing the air toward the magistrate. "We saw him this morning, and he had both hands! Only a cleric of your power could ask the gods for such a favor. And they granted it to you."

Lexos stood stone silent for a moment, steaming at Kellach. "Even if this were so—that I decided to show mercy to a penitent who promised to mend his ways and dedicate his life to the cause of St. Cuthbert—that hardly means I asked him to kill Zendric."

Kellach spat on the ground. "Kruncher couldn't have managed it on his own. You've been to Zendric's tower dozens of times. I've seen you there myself. You saw the spiritkeeper there and knew you could tell Kruncher to use it on Zendric. Didn't you?"

Lexos snorted in disgust. "This is preposterous. Of course I've been to Zendric's home. We are friends. We are leaders of the city. We hold counsel with each other on matters many and varied."

While Lexos spoke, he moved toward Kellach. The apprentice circled around so that he was on the other side of the slabs, next to Moyra and Driskoll.

"You knew how the spiritkeeper worked," Kellach continued. "But you lacked the guts to work it yourself. Instead, your persuaded poor Kruncher—who I can't believe I'm actually sorry for—to do the job for you. It was that or rot in prison!"

"Be silent, boy!" Lexos thundered. "You have no idea who you're dealing with."

"Of course I do," Kellach said. "You're a jealous, pathetic shell of a creature. You hide behind the righteousness of your frock to kill people whose air you're not fit to share!"

Lexos's face turned a bright red as Kellach spoke. When the young apprentice was finished, the magistrate said, "By all that's holy, I have had enough!"

The three kids stood frozen in horror. Lexos leered across the body lying before him.

"You're a clever boy, Kellach," the magistrate said, "too clever for your own good. No one else in town has a clue. Your father wastes his time poking around after common criminals. As if any of them could have killed a wizard like Zendric on his own!"

Lexos cackled. "No, child. You're right. It was me all along. I did it. I made the deal with this Kruncher. I told him how to break into Zendric's tower and how to use this 'spiritkeeper,' as you call it.

"In fact," Lexos went on, calmer now, but ever more cruel, "I have you three to thank for this. I'd been searching for the right person for the job for months. I almost thought I'd have to handle the matter myself, but your antics last night brought Kruncher right to me. You practically threw him into my lap."

Driskoll looked up at Kellach. Tears welled in Kellach's eyes, and Lexos laughed at the sight. Driskoll knew these weren't tears of shame but frustration. Kellach wanted to make Lexos pay, but Driskoll couldn't see how. Driskoll looked past Kellach to Moyra, who stood there wide-eyed and terrified.

"Why?" Kellach said. "That's what I don't understand. Why?"

"Power, boy," Lexos said grimly. "It's about power. Since the last of the Knights of the Silver Dragon were killed in the Sundering, Curston has lacked strong leadership. Those of us who care about the city have worked together to save it, but we need a single, decisive ruler.

"It was clear from the start that I was the right person for the job, but Zendric and his cronies on the ruling council stonewalled me at every step.

"Now that the city's defenses are stable—now that your father has done such a wonderful job—the old wizard is expendable. It was clear that if I was ever to ascend to Curston's throne, this 'mage of the people' would have to go."

"And with him out of the way now, the city is yours," said Kellach.

"Precisely."

"And if any others should stand up against your power play?"

Lexos grinned savagely. "They will meet the same fate. If Zendric couldn't stop me, then no one will. They'll all fall in line, even your father. If brave Torin won't toe the line, I'll declare him a traitor and have him hanged from the top of the Westgate at dusk!"

"Never!" Driskoll shouted. He started to jump over the bier to strangle the magistrate with his own hands. Lexos uttered a word and gestured at him, and the boy found himself frozen in place, unable to move a single muscle.

Lexos laughed. "So the little one finally shows some spirit. So like your mother."

"You'll never get away with this," Kellach said. "Our father will find you out, and the entire town will assemble against you."

"And who will tell him of my indiscretions?" Lexos asked. "You? I'm afraid I can't allow that to happen."

"You can't just kill us. You'd practically have to cremate us along with Zendric to destroy all the evidence."

Lexos's face lit up. "Once again, boy, you are too clever for your own good. That's an excellent idea." With that, he turned and walked out of the cremation chamber.

Moyra screamed. Driskoll would have too if he'd been able to speak.

"You can't do this!" Kellach shouted. "Our father will come looking for us!"

"After what he thinks you did today?" Lexos asked. "Ha! I don't have to do anything other than lock this door. When the cremators stoke the ovens tomorrow to burn that body, they'll take care of the problem for me."

"You said you'd hold a ceremony for Zendric."

"I lied."

With that, Lexos slid the door shut, and the three friends found themselves enveloped in total darkness. Kellach scrambled over the stone slabs and threw himself against the door, but he was too late. By the time he got there, Lexos had already locked them inside.

CHAPTER

21

The spell on Driskoll wore off a short while later. When it did, the boy let loose with the scream that had been trapped inside of him.

At that moment, the fact that Lexos had killed Zendric didn't mean a thing to Driskoll. The only thing that mattered was that he was stuck in a pitch-black room. The next thing he would probably see would be the flames that flooded the room just before he died.

Someone reached out and grabbed Driskoll by the shoulder. He screamed again, afraid that Lexos had decided that he didn't want to wait for the kids to be dead.

It was Kellach.

"It's okay," he said. "This is going exactly as I planned."

The words stopped Driskoll cold. "You planned this?" he shouted. "Are you crazy?"

"Kellach," Moyra said, her voice unusually calm. "If you have a plan here, could you share it with us?" Driskoll figured she'd had about all she could take and was inches from entirely shutting down.

"Sure. Just hold on for a moment." Kellach said something, and then a bright light burst out of the darkness. It was shaped like a knife—Kellach's knife.

Kellach held his knife out over his head like a torch. It shone from pommel to tip as if it burned from within. "That's better. We have to work quickly though. This won't last long."

"That's not going to get us out of here," Driskoll said.

"That won't," Kellach said. He held up the spiritkeeper like a trophy. "But this will."

"It didn't work the first time!" Moyra said. "How's it supposed to work now?"

"I didn't really activate it before," Kellach said. "I just faked it."

"What?" Driskoll and Moyra said in unison.

"Even before his slip, I didn't trust Lexos entirely. Imagine if I'd have restored Zendric while Lexos was standing there over him. Lexos would have executed Zendric on the spot, and us along with him."

"Yes!" Moyra said. "So now you can put Zendric's soul back in his body, and he can get us out of here."

Driskoll let a bit of hope into his heart. "Are you sure?"

"Nothing's ever for sure," Kellach said with an infectious smile, "but I'll put my last copper on the most powerful wizard in Curston any day."

Moyra reached over and grabbed the top of the sheet covering the body on the bier. "Ready?" she asked.

Kellach handed Driskoll the knife. He held it as high as he could over the body. He wanted to give Kellach every chance possible to make this work right.

Kellach grasped the spiritkeeper in both hands. Then he

drew in a deep breath and blew it out. He nodded at Moyra, and she drew back the sheet with a flourish.

The body under the sheet wasn't Zendric.

It was Kruncher.

Kruncher was bruised all over his chest and face, and the hand that he'd lost once already was missing again. Even in death, he looked like he had a chip on his shoulder.

Kellach sat down on the floor and put the spiritkeeper in his lap and his head in his hands. "That's why Lexos wasn't worried about the spiritkeeper working," he said quietly.

Moyra shook her head and backed away from Kruncher's corpse until she hit the wall behind her. As she went, she said, "No, no, no, no, no!"

"This is some kind of cosmic joke, right?" Driskoll said. "This can't be the end. It can't!" He knelt next to his brother and shook him by the shoulders. "Come on, Kellach! There's another way out of this, right? Right?"

Kellach let his hands fall onto the spiritkeeper in his lap. His eyes suddenly looked sunken and tired. "Just give me a minute," he said quietly. "Let me think."

Driskoll stood up and scratched his head for a moment. "I've got it!" he said. "We can just wait for the workers to come in tomorrow and then bang on the door until they hear us. They wouldn't just stoke the furnaces without checking here first, right?"

Moyra shook her head. "That's a rotten idea. Lexos is out there, and those workers follow his orders. What do you think will happen?"

"If you have a better idea, don't hold back."

"How about we destroy the spiritkeeper?"

"You're kidding, right? Wouldn't that kill Zendric?" Driskoll thought about it for a moment and turned to Kellach. "Well? Would it?"

Kellach got to his feet. He was still a bit shaken, but he was beginning to rally. "I'm not sure." He scratched his chin as he stared down at the spiritkeeper in his hands.

"My best guess," Kellach said, "is that, yes, destroying this thing would free Zendric's soul. If the soul can then find his body in time, Zendric would come back to life. If he can hear and understand any of this, he might even realize where we are and come to rescue us."

"That's an awful lot of ifs," Driskoll said.

"But if it's our only option," Moyra said. "I say we take a vote on it."

"No." Kellach shook his head. "I have a better idea." He handed the spiritkeeper to Driskoll.

"What am I supposed to do with this?" Driskoll asked.

"Use it," Kellach said, "on me."

Driskoll gaped at him. "You can't be serious."

"No!" said Moyra. "It makes perfect sense. With Zendric in Kellach's body, he can use his magic to get us out of here."

Driskoll looked at Kellach. "If that's so, why don't you just use it on me?"

"I'm the only one here with any magical training. My voice has been trained to speak the words. My hands know how to make the gestures. I don't know for sure if that will make a difference, but I'd rather not take the chance."

Driskoll nodded, still not sure he believed it. "How do I work this?"

"Just aim it toward me and say the word inscribed on the bottom."

Driskoll looked under the spiritkeeper and then back at Kellach. "I can't read that."

"It's in Draconic," Kellach said. "Let me pronounce it for you." He whispered it to Driskoll, then made his younger brother repeat it back to him over and over until he was satisfied Driskoll had it right.

"That light's going to run out any minute now, isn't it?" said Driskoll.

Kellach nodded. "Let's get this over with."

Driskoll pointed the spiritkeeper at Kellach and looked him in the eye. Before Driskoll could say anything, Kellach reached over and hugged his brother. "Good luck," Kellach said as he released Driskoll.

Driskoll gazed into his brother's eyes again as he pointed the spiritkeeper at Kellach. "You too," Driskoll said. Then he said the word.

"*Animamedere*."

CHAPTER

22

The now-familiar vortex of glowing smoke swirled out of the golden globe. Thick clouds of gray gas surrounded Kellach. Driskoll could barely see his brother through the smoke. Then all at once the smoke flew back inside the spiritkeeper and the air was clear again. Kellach stood there in front of Moyra and Driskoll, his eyes closed tight.

"Kellach?" Driskoll asked quietly.

He didn't respond.

"Zendric?"

Kellach's eyes opened slowly. They seemed older and wiser than before. "Driskoll?" Kellach's voice said. His eyes looked the other boy up and down. "You've grown taller." Kellach looked at his arms. "Or I've grown shorter." He hesitated a moment. "Ah. I'm in Kellach's body, aren't I?"

Moyra and Driskoll nodded.

Kellach smiled. "And where are we?"

Moyra and Driskoll both started babbling at once. Kellach quickly put up a hand and said, "One at a time, please! I would guess that we do not have much time to lose. Driskoll?"

"We're in a cremation chamber under the House of the Dead, and Lexos left us here to die after Kellach figured out that he was the one who hired Kruncher to steal your soul." Driskoll looked down at his hands and realized he was still holding the spiritkeeper. "Using this!"

"Ah," Kellach said. "That explains much." He reached up to scratch his chin, and Driskoll realized where Kellach had picked up that habit. "And how long have we been in here?"

"Minutes," Moyra said. "I'll bet that Lexos is still in the building. If we hurry, we can catch him!"

"Well, then," Kellach said. "We had better get started."

Just then the light from Kellach's knife went out. Moyra let out a little scream of surprise.

"That will not do," Kellach said. He muttered something, and a light equivalent to three torches burst out of the knife. "Much better," he said as he picked up the knife and handed it to Driskoll.

"Now, about that door," Kellach said, turning to face it. "I assume it is locked."

Moyra and Driskoll nodded.

"Fair enough." Kellach spoke another of those strange words that always seemed to slip right through the listener's head. "Try it now," he said.

Moyra dashed forward and pulled at the door. It slid aside easily. Driskoll stuffed the spiritkeeper back into Kellach's pack and slung the bag over his shoulder.

Moyra and Driskoll rushed into the hallway. The air there wasn't much less stale than that in the cremation chamber, but it tasted of freedom and life, and the kids gulped it down.

Kellach strode out of the chamber, rubbing his hands together and cracking his knuckles. "Now," he said, "let's find Lexos. I believe he and I need to have a short conversation."

The three hustled through the corridors until they found the stairwell leading back up to the foyer. Kellach led the way through the maze like he was walking through his own home.

When the trio reached the foyer, it was empty. Kellach marched over to the front door and tried to open it, but it was locked. He spoke one of those words again, and the door swung wide at his touch.

The two guards standing outside the door yelped as it opened behind them. "Hey!" the younger one yelled. "Lexos said he sent you home."

Kellach ignored him. "Lexos," he said in a commanding tone, "where is he?"

The elder guard pointed at a cloaked shape walking across the square that fronted the House of the Dead. "That's him right there."

"Lexos!" Kellach shouted.

The magistrate turned back and saw the three kids trotting across the square toward him, leaving the guards on the steps behind. He strode out to meet them in the center of the square, as far as possible from the everburning torches ringing the area.

"By Cuthbert's cudgel!" Lexos said. "You children are as stupid as you are annoying." He grabbed Kellach by the shoulders with clawlike hands. "You should have run home to your father while you had the chance, boy. Instead, I'm going to kill you all on the spot."

"How do you plan to get away with it this time?" asked Driskoll.

Lexos spoke in a sad tone, but through gritted teeth. "They came at me. They must have been possessed by a rogue spirit."

Lexos released Kellach and began chanting a prayer to the gods. Driskoll didn't understand much of it, but he caught the words "strike dead" somewhere in there. Lexos's hands began to crackle and glow with raw power.

As the magistrate spoke, Moyra and Driskoll crept backward, although they both knew they could never run fast enough to escape. Kellach stepped closer, speaking in the strange tongue of magic again, and made a dismissive gesture at Lexos. The power suddenly drained from the magistrate's hands.

Startled, Lexos stared at Kellach. "How?" he asked. "A boy of your—" He cut himself off short and peered into Kellach's eyes.

"By the gods," Lexos whispered. "Zendric?"

Kellach flashed a savage grin at the magistrate. "I have only one thing to say to you, 'old friend.'" He spat a single, horrible syllable that Driskoll's brain mercifully refused to understand.

At the sound of the word, Lexos dropped to his knees on the hard cobblestones of the square, clutching at his ears. He looked up at Kellach, his face contorted in a mixture of confusion and fear.

Kellach let loose a punch that smashed into Lexos's nose and knocked him flat on his back. He flexed his fingers, and said, "I hope Kellach will forgive me that indulgence. I have wanted to do that for a long time."

Then Kellach looked at Moyra and Driskoll. "Do either of you have rope?"

Driskoll reached into Kellach's pack and pulled out the coil of thin rope stowed there. Kellach kneeled down and used it to hog-tie Lexos tightly. As he worked, he asked, "How about a handkerchief? I need a gag."

Driskoll pulled out the remnants of the shirt he'd torn to pieces to mend Durmok's wounds.

"Perfect," Kellach smiled. He stuffed one piece of the shirt into the magistrate's mouth, then used another strip to tie the first piece into place.

Lexos was starting to recover. He tried spitting out the gag, but it was securely in place. With his hands and feet bound behind him, he had to settle for screaming into the fabric, which muffled the sound nicely. Driskoll couldn't help but laugh.

"What do you think you're doing?" said a voice from over Driskoll's shoulder. He turned to see the two watchers standing over them, their swords drawn.

Kellach leaped to his feet and was nearly stabbed for his trouble. "My good watchers," he said, "I believe I can explain everything—with the help of my young friends, that is." With that, he nodded at Moyra and Driskoll. "If you could call the captain of the guard first, I would appreciate it. I hate repeating myself. I'm sure Torin would understand."

"You expect us to follow the orders of three kids while you stand over the body of the magistrate?" the younger watcher asked.

Kellach spoke another of those strange words and flicked his hands, which immediately burst into flames. By the way he waved them around, it was clear the fire wasn't hurting him, but Driskoll could feel their heat well enough. The watchers could too.

"Not everything is as it seems here," Kellach said. "You would do well to heed my request."

The elder watcher looked at his partner and said, "Go. Hurry."

Soon, Torin was in the square with a dozen watchers. Kellach's hands were no longer burning, but the watchers maintained a respectful distance from him as he stood over the still-struggling Lexos.

"What in the name of the gods?" Torin began.

Kellach cut him off with a wave of his hand. "Torin, I do not have time for this. Your sons and this young lady have done me a great service, but I would like to get back to my own body—old and battered as it is—as quickly as possible."

Torin's jaw dropped. "Zendric?" He shook his head. "Kellach, if this is your idea of a prank . . . "

"On my honor as a Silver Dragon," Kellach said.

Torin nodded, weighing the situation in his mind. "All right, Zendric," he said. "Let's do what we must. And if this is a joke, whoever is in that body will get the hiding of his life."

Kellach pointed down at Lexos. "Here is the culprit behind the scenes of this drama," he said. "He is too powerful to be let loose again. I ask that your watchers keep him bound and gagged until we return."

Torin looked to Gwinton, who was standing beside him. "As you wish," the dwarf said with relish.

Torin, Moyra, and Driskoll followed Kellach back into the House of the Dead. He led them down again into the passages under the building, straight to the second cremation chamber. The door was locked, but Kellach opened it with a word.

Inside, Torin and the kids found a covered corpse. Kellach pulled back the sheet to reveal Zendric's body. He sighed softly. "I look so old," he said to himself. He reached out and caressed the wrinkled forehead.

Then Kellach turned to Driskoll and asked, "Do you have it?"

Driskoll reached into the pack and pulled out the spiritkeeper.

"It was you who used it last?" Kellach asked.

Driskoll nodded.

"You may have the honor again."

Kellach closed his eyes. Driskoll pointed the spiritkeeper at him and spoke the word, and the vortex of glowing smoke swirled between Kellach and the device. Driskoll heard Torin gasp at the sight, and he looked back to see Moyra holding Torin's hand.

When Driskoll turned his attention back to Kellach, the smoke had returned to the spiritkeeper once again.

"Did it work?" Kellach asked. Driskoll nodded at him with a grin.

Kellach looked around to see Torin and Moyra standing behind his brother. He smiled broadly at them. "Hello, Dad," he said. "I hope you're not too mad."

Torin shook his head, amazed. "No," he said. "But we're going to have a long talk after this." He looked at Driskoll as well. "All three of us."

Driskoll handed the spiritkeeper to Kellach. The apprentice shot his brother a questioning look, and Driskoll pointed over his shoulder. Kellach turned and saw Zendric's body laid out on the stone slab.

Kellach pointed the device at his instructor's corpse and said the word. The smoke leaped out from the globe one more time and enveloped Zendric's body. For a moment, Driskoll wasn't sure that it was working. He feared that Zendric's soul had been too long gone from its home.

The smoke stopped swirling again. Everyone held their breath and waited. Just when Driskoll thought he could take it no more, the old wizard sat up and smiled.

"Many thanks, my friends," Zendric said. "Many thanks."

CHAPTER

23

My mom still doesn't believe a word of it," Moyra said the next morning as she, Kellach, and Driskoll walked Curston's sunlit streets. "I don't know if she ever will." She smiled. "I'm going to visit my dad later today and tell him the whole thing though. He'll love it!"

The streets of the city were bustling with their same old activity: children played in doorways, parents hung out washing to dry, workers strode off to their jobs. It was just the same as it had ever been, but today it all somehow seemed more precious than before.

As they strolled along, Driskoll noticed Kellach holding back a little. He had his hands in his pockets, and his head hung low.

"What's the matter?" Driskoll asked. "You should be in a great mood!"

Kellach grimaced. "I'm happy enough, I suppose."

"You suppose?" Moyra said, her eyes glinting. "What could be wrong on a day like this?"

Kellach hesitated for a moment. "I'm not studying magic any more."

"Since when?" Moyra said, indignant. "Talk about a waste! You've got a real talent for it."

Kellach nodded. "But I don't have a teacher anymore."

Moyra laughed. "But a lot has happened since then. A lot! Zendric will take you back in for sure." She saw the uncertain looks on her friends' faces, then added weakly, "Won't he?"

Kellach shrugged as they kept walking. "I suppose we'll find out."

When the kids neared Zendric's tower, they saw that his door stood open once again. They looked at each other and then broke into a run.

The trio burst in through the open doorway to find Zendric sitting in a comfortable chair, reading a book. As he turned the pages, his belongings were somehow picking themselves up off the floor and finding their old homes. A broom moved by itself, sweeping the shattered things into a pile near the hearth. The place was almost back to its old self.

Zendric finished the page he was reading, then looked up and smiled. "Welcome," he said. "Come in. I'm just tidying up." He noticed the kids staring at the work going on all around him, then waved his hand. "Oh, don't worry about them," he said. "They'll stay out of your way."

The old wizard stood up and gestured for the kids to take the chairs near him. They accepted and settled in.

"I was worried when we were walking up here," Driskoll said as he sat down. "With the door open again like that."

Zendric smiled. "I just wanted to air the place out a bit. Cleaning like this stirs up a great deal of dust. Besides," he said, his voice dropping to a stage-whisper, "the place smelled just a bit of orc."

The wizard walked over to the pile of trash near the hearth. He examined it for a moment, found what he wanted, and reached down and plucked it from the mess.

"I'm glad you three are here," Zendric said. "Torin is sure to insist on a proper ceremony later, but I wanted to let you know what we have planned."

The three friends looked at each other and then at Zendric. "What are you talking about?" Driskoll asked.

The old wizard smiled, then walked over to them. "Hold out your hands," he said.

The kids complied, and Zendric placed something into each of their outstretched palms. Driskoll looked in his hand. It was one of the silver dragon pins he had seen scattered across Zendric's floor yesterday morning.

"These are the insignia of the Knights of the Silver Dragon," Zendric said.

Moyra gasped. Kellach and Driskoll looked on the pins in awe.

"Thank you!" Driskoll said. "This is an amazing honor."

"You must learn not to interrupt, young Driskoll," Zendric said. "I am not yet finished."

Driskoll clamped his mouth shut.

"Thanks to you, Lexos is no longer a thorn in my side. I am already preparing a special cell for him in the city prison, and the Church of St. Cuthbert will soon strip him of his office. Those who supported him on the ruling council remain, but they are cowed by the scandal surrounding his attempt on my life. No one wishes to stand with an assassin. The council will meet soon to select a replacement for Lexos."

"But—" Driskoll said before cutting himself off. Zendric

nodded at him to continue. "But with Lexos out of the way, you could run the city yourself."

"Possibly," Zendric chuckled. "If I were interested in such things. Ruling Curston holds no lure for me. I only wish to help its people. A strong ruling council is a good means for that. In the meantime, however, I must confess I've used a bit of my newfound pull to resurrect an enterprise I'd long since given up on."

Zendric paused for a moment to let his words sink in. "I spoke with Torin this morning," Zendric continued. "He was impressed with how you three handled yourselves. And as you boys know, impressing your father is not easily done."

Kellach and Driskoll nodded.

"I had an idea that I proposed to him, and he gave it his full blessing." The wizard turned serious.

"Curston has had a long, hard history. For a good part of that, I and a small circle of friends stood as the city's heroes, ready to lay down our lives in the defense of hearth and home. Most of those heroes are now long gone. We were dying out before the Sundering of the Seal, and that tragic event led to the loss of the rest. Except for me.

"As old as I am, I sometimes forget that things can change, that just as the seasons cycle through each year, a city can renew itself. When there is a need for new heroes, they arise like flowers in the spring." Zendric smiled. "Torin and I have decided to recognize that fact finally. As the last surviving member of my old order, it's up to me to help renew it.

"Curston needs the Knights of the Silver Dragon again," Zendric said. "And so now, it has you."

Driskoll almost burst out of his seat. "Are you serious?" he asked, clutching the pin before him like it might try to fly away. "You're inducting us into the Knights of the Silver Dragon?"

Zendric nodded, and Driskoll jumped out of his seat. He let out a cheer that could have awakened the dead. Kellach and Moyra joined in, and the three of them celebrated until they were hoarse.

"Congratulations, my friends," Zendric said, giving the kids a smile both warm and wide. "It is an honor well deserved."

Swept up in the moment, the kids raced over to Zendric and wrapped him in a large, communal hug. He laughed and held back for a moment, then returned the embrace in kind.

"Now, friends," Zendric said when the kids finally released him. "You should run along and meet up with Torin at the Watchers' Hall. He needs you for the formal announcement."

"Aren't you coming along?" Driskoll asked.

Zendric grinned and tousled Driskoll's hair. "Presently. I have a few details to finish with here first." The room was almost entirely back in order, and the broom was pushing the last bits of dust into the pile on the hearth.

Kellach, Moyra, and Driskoll scrambled for the exit.

"But we'll see you there for sure?" Moyra said as they reached the door.

Zendric nodded. "I'll be along in a moment. I have to get things ready for my classes. I'm resuming them tomorrow."

Driskoll glanced at Kellach, who was staring out the doorway. The smile fled from the older boy's face.

"I'll expect you first thing in the morning, Kellach," said Zendric.

The apprentice whipped around, a grin growing on his face.

"After all," said Zendric, "I don't want my star pupil to be late."

Kellach nodded at Zendric, nearly bursting with pride, but managing to somehow hold it in. Moyra and Driskoll clapped him on the back and pulled him out into the street.

The three friends ran out the door and down the street toward Watchers' Hall. The sunlight shone down on the city and bathed them in its warm, renewing rays. They laughed the whole way there.

KNIGHTS OF THE SILVER DRAGON

A young thief.
A wizard's apprentice.
A twelve-year-old boy.
Meet the Knights of
the Silver Dragon!

SECRET OF THE SPIRITKEEPER
Matt Forbeck

Can Moyra, Kellach, and Driskoll unlock the secret of the
spiritkeeper in time to rescue their beloved wizard friend?

August 2004

RIDDLE IN STONE
Ree Soesbee

Will the Knights unravel the statue's riddle
before more people turn to stone?

August 2004

SIGN OF THE SHAPESHIFTER
Dale Donovan and Linda Johns

Can Kellach and Driskoll find the shapeshifter
before he ruins their father?

October 2004

EYE OF FORTUNE
Denise R. Graham

Does the fortuneteller's prophecy spell doom
for the Knights? Or unheard-of treasure?

December 2004

For ages 8 and up

JOIN THE

AND RECEIVE A COLLECTIBLE
SILVER DRAGON MINIATURE!

YOUR SILVER DRAGON MINIATURE IS FREE!

Follow these steps to become a **Knights of the Silver Dragon** member.
Important: If you are under 13, one of your parents will need to sign this
form. If your parent does not sign this form, we won't be able to enroll
you in KNIGHTS OF THE SILVER DRAGON.

1) Read this.
By filling out this form you are enrolling in **Knights of the Silver Dragon**.
This will make you eligible to receive:

• A silver dragon miniature and other collectibles;
• Information about upcoming books;
• And other cool information about the **Knights of the Silver Dragon!**

2) Please provide your contact information.

First Name: _____   Phone: _____

Last Name: _____   Email: _____

Address: _____   ☐ Male ☐ Female

City: _____   Date of Birth (month/day/year):

State/Province: _____   _____

Zip/Postal Code: _____   Country* (check one): ☐ U.S.A. ☐ Canada

*Offer valid in the U.S. and Canada.

3) Get your parents to sign this form after reading the "Parents" information if you are under 13.

Parent/Guardian's Printed Name: _____

Parent/Guardian's Signature: _____

4) Send completed and signed membership/consent form to:

Knights of the Silver Dragon
C/O KP Fulfillment House
20014 70th Avenue South
Kent, WA 98032

Your Silver Dragon Miniature costs nothing!
Send your membership and consent form in now!

Limit one **Knights of the Silver Dragon** membership and dragon miniature collectible per person. Miniature offer valid while supplies last. Allow 6 to 8 weeks for delivery.

PARENTS:

Your child would like to register for Knights of the Silver Dragon membership from Wizards of the Coast. When you send in this form, your child will be sent membership materials including a dragon miniature collectible (while supplies last), information about upcoming books published by Mirrorstone Books, and other printed materials related to Knights of the Silver Dragon, Mirrorstone, and Wizards of the Coast. From time to time, your child may also be sent other physical mailings and emails. In the future, membership in Knights of the Silver Dragon may also include access to a special area of the Wizards of the Coast web site, where your child may be able to change his contact information and participate in online surveys. Before we can allow your child's personal and demographic information to be viewed and modified online, we want to notify you about our online information collection practices and obtain your permission. We ask that you first read through the "Note to Parents" in the Wizards Website Privacy Statement (http://www.wizards.com/parents), which identifies the personal information that Wizards of the Coast collects from children online and the way we handle such information. If you cannot connect to our web site, our customer service team can provide you with the information and answer any other questions (800-424-6496).

When you have finished reading the parental information materials referenced above, please sign this registration form where it says "Parent/Guardian's Signature."

Please note that once you have signed and sent us this form, you always have the ability to: (i.) review your child's personal information collected online; (ii.) request that we delete your child's personal information online; (iii.) stop us from further using or collecting additional personal information online about your child without gaining new permission from you. To do so, please contact us using the information provided above.